Her gaze flicked to the olive groves she could see from the window, then shifted back to the painting again. She could almost hear the silvery leaves rustling in the breeze, had never realized how fascinating an olive tree could be.

Señor Goyo had been tending them from boyhood, extracting from their fruit the rich oil revered by men over the centuries. The thought of him engaged in something so important throughout his whole life had a strange effect on her, moving her to tears for a reason she couldn't comprehend.

To her dismay he'd come back in the room with her suitcase and his flowers, catching her in another emotional moment.

She heard his sharp intake of breath before he lowered her bag to the floor and walked over to her. "What am I going to do with you?" he asked in a husky tone.

Jillian knew what she wanted him to do. She wanted him to hold her in his arms, kiss her, caress her. But that would be the worst thing she could do—for herself, and him.

From city girl—to corporate wife!

They're working side by side, nine to five....
But no matter how hard these couples
try to keep their relationships strictly professional,
romance is undeniably on the agenda!

But will a date in the office diary lead to an
appointment at the altar?

Find out in this exciting miniseries.

If you love office-romance stories—
next month look out for

Hired: The Boss's Bride
by Ally Blake
in October 2008

REBECCA WINTERS

Crazy about her Spanish Boss

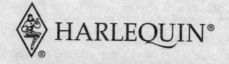

TORONTO • NEW YORK • LONDON
AMSTERDAM • PARIS • SYDNEY • HAMBURG
STOCKHOLM • ATHENS • TOKYO • MILAN • MADRID
PRAGUE • WARSAW • BUDAPEST • AUCKLAND

ISBN-13: 978-0-373-17539-0
ISBN-10:   0-373-17539-6

CRAZY ABOUT HER SPANISH BOSS

First North American Publication 2008.

Rebecca Winters, whose family of four children has now swelled to include three beautiful grandchildren, lives in Salt Lake City, Utah, in the land of the Rocky Mountains. With canyons and high alpine meadows full of wildflowers, she never runs out of places to explore. They, plus her favorite vacation spots in Europe, often end up as backgrounds for her romance novels, because writing is her passion, along with her family and church. Rebecca loves to hear from her readers. If you wish to e-mail her, please visit her Web site at www.cleanromances.com.

CHAPTER ONE

"A COGNAC IN CELEBRATION, Don Remi?"

Remigio Alfonso de Vargas y Goyo sat back in the leather chair with his long legs crossed at the ankles. He disliked being addressed as if he was a royal relic. It was archaic. Remi was a man of the soil. In this day and age a title was absurd. He studied his loyal accountant with a jaundiced eye. "Of what?"

The tidy older man approaching seventy years of age poured himself a drink. "Your business has surpassed what it was befo—" He stopped short of finishing the sentence. A slight flush tinged his cheeks before he looked away and swallowed the swirling amber liquid. "Well, let's just say Soleado Goyo is once again on its way to giving your competitors a major headache."

"Don't count my chickens too fast, Luis. We're in the middle of another drought cycle with no end in sight. The olive groves are always hit hardest. You know that." With the loss of the Spanish colonies in the 1850s, Spain's wealth had diminished and the Goyos had been forced to work for a living. Gone were the fortunes of the previous Dukes of Toledo from which the Goyo line had descended.

"So you diversify in anticipation."

His caustic laugh resounded in the room. "Like my father

once did? It ended up being the costliest mistake of his life and drove both my parents to an early grave. I'm afraid I'm a purist."

Luis shrugged. "It was a mere suggestion, Remi. You're the expert. Far be it from me to tell you anything."

"Your long association with Papa gives you the right."

"Nevertheless I'm only good with numbers."

"Which you do very well indeed," he muttered.

"Gracias."

Remi levered his tall, powerful body from the chair. After two long, grueling years of blood and sweat he'd finally paid off the last of his late father's bank debt. It had saved his family's honor and reputation in the region. However, he'd still dreaded this meeting with Luis. Each time he drove to Toledo on business it called up dark, bitter memories he only managed to suppress as long as he stayed too busy to think.

Right now he could feel the acid bitterness of betrayal scorching his insides like a river of molten magma. Once its journey started, no power could stave it off. At times like this he wasn't fit company for anyone, least of all Luis who'd been his cheering section for as long as he could remember. The older man deserved better.

In a few swift strides he reached the door, anxious to get back home.

"Remi?"

He turned his dark head in Luis's direction. *"Sí?"*

"I'm very proud of what you've accomplished. Your father would be proud, too."

Not if his papa had already turned over in his grave.

Remi sincerely hoped his parent had no way of knowing how close his thirty-three-year-old son had come to losing everything five generations of Goyos had worked so hard to achieve.

If Luis didn't recognize Remi anymore, that was no surprise. The man who stared back at Remi in the mirror every morning couldn't possibly be Luis Goyo's son—his firstborn offspring whose appalling lack of judgment in his personal life still continued to blacken Remi's world.

He gave Luis an unsmiling nod and left the office. In an economy of movement he descended the two steep flights of stairs to the narrow street where he'd parked his black sedan.

As a boy he'd been able to walk beneath the gothic arches of these ancient streets without feeling as if he was part of a parade crowd. Since that time tourists from around the globe had discovered Toledo and now flowed in and out of the city no matter the season. When at all possible, he went out of his way to avoid them. They were more stifling than the heat that had come to the heart of central Spain.

July brought an unforgiving summer sun that portended dry lightning and fires. A lick of flame could make a torch out of a gnarled olive tree. Maybe one day it would mistake *him* for one of them. Why not?

It was a hard life fewer and fewer owners of the large latifundia chose to embrace, but it was *his* life. Though every dream of his had been destroyed, the estate he'd inherited remained, giving him the last remaining reason to get up in the morning.

He removed his lightweight suit jacket and tie. After tossing them in the backseat, he got behind the wheel and started the engine. Soon he was winding his way past Moorish walls to the outskirts. For a while the road bordered the Tagus River, then opened onto the solitary plain where the traffic had thinned.

As he sped south, the great Alcázar of Toledo, standing like a sentinel on the granite hill behind him, disappeared. At three in the afternoon there were few vehicles on the road. While his car ate up the kilometers, he felt his taut muscles relax knowing that inside of fifteen minutes he'd be back on the estate with a ton of work to do before going to bed.

Work saved his life.

During the day physical labor kept him from reliving the past. Unfortunately the long dark hours of the night brought the demons he was forced to wrestle with over and over again. When he awakened in the mornings, he was emotionally exhausted.

Deep in his torturous thoughts he was barely cognizant of a car in the distance. It had just rounded the long curve and was coming in his direction. The driver must have seen the stray bull crossing the highway at the same time he did.

Remi's speed was such that he knew it would be too dangerous to brake, but the other driver obeyed the opposite instinct and the car swerved. In a split second it was on a collision course for him. He yanked the steering wheel to the right to escape impact. The other driver overcorrected to avoid him. To his horror the other car rolled behind him onto the shoulder and landed on the passenger side, coming to a stop.

He brought his car to a halt, then shot out and raced to the blue compact car whose tires were still spinning in the air. The front and rear windows had been broken. Glass lay everywhere. He looked inside. The driver was the only occupant. A woman. She was moaning.

Gracias a Dios, she was alive! The seat belt had kept her from being thrown.

Remi tried to the open the door, but couldn't. He reached in to undo the lock. "You're going to be all right, *Senora*," he assured her in his native tongue.

"Help me…" came her anguished cry. "My eye— I can't see—" Though she spoke passable Spanish, she was definitely an American.

"Be as still as you can," he responded firmly in accented English. "Don't touch your eye or you'll make it worse. I'm going to lift you out. Let me do all the work."

As he reached around to undo her seat belt, he saw blood oozing down the right side of her face. Her shoulder-length blond hair was spattered with it.

He gathered her slight weight in his arms, aware of her flowery fragrance as he carried her to safety and laid her on the ground with as much care as possible. "I'll have you to a hospital shortly. Don't move."

"I won't," she whispered shakily in English through lips made bluish-white from shock. The pallor of her face and the fists her hands made let him know her pain was excruciating, but instead of screaming hysterically she showed a rare courage he could only admire.

No doubt a piece of flying metal or glass had caused the injury. He pulled the cell phone from his trouser pocket and phoned the police. After a quick explanation from him, they promised to send a medical helicopter immediately.

After the call was made, he rang his foreman, Paco, and explained what had happened. He told him to get one of the staff and come for his car. Paco could wait for the police and give them the details. Remi planned to accompany the woman to the hospital. Once he'd seen to her care, he'd talk to the police himself.

In his gut he felt responsible for the crash. It might have been avoided if his mind hadn't been somewhere else.

As he clicked off, he noticed several cars stopping to offer help. The injured woman reached for his free hand. "No people. Please—" she implored. Her ringless fingers clutched his so hard that her nails dug into his palms, but he didn't mind. Her control was nothing short of amazing.

He told the other drivers the police were coming and waved them on. In another minute they were alone again.

"What's your name?"

"J-Jillian Gray."

An unusual first name. He liked the sound of it on her tongue.

"Do you have a husband or a boyfriend I can call?"

"No."

"Are you here with a friend or family member?"

"No." Every word had to be an effort.

"Hold on a few more minutes, Jillian. I can hear the helicopter coming. You'll be out of your pain soon."

"Is my eye still there?"

Madre de Dios. The fear in her voice killed him. "Of course. Everything's going to be fine." It *had* to be. "The bleeding has stopped. Don't cry. You wouldn't want the salt from your tears to irritate it."

"No." Her softly rounded chin wobbled. The sight of it reminded him how brave she was being. His insides quivered in response.

There were a dozen questions he wanted answers to, but he knew the hospital staff would get the pertinent information from her. Right now she was in too much pain to be interrogated.

"The helicopter's here."

"My purse—"

"Don't worry about that now." He'd leave it for the police, who would need to see her passport. When they were through with the investigation, he'd get it back from them. "The important thing is to take care of you. I'll make certain all your belongings are returned to you."

"Thank you," she whispered.

Three medical personnel jumped down and hurried over to

them. The next few minutes passed in a blur as she was examined and lifted on to a gurney. Remi followed as they transported her to the helicopter.

No sooner had he climbed inside and they'd taken off than he heard sirens. Out of the window he saw one of the estate cars with the logo approaching the accident scene from the opposite direction. Paco was now there to sort everything out with the police.

To his relief they were giving the woman antibiotics and painkillers through an IV. Already she was calmer. They'd braced her neck so she couldn't move her head. He was glad they hadn't tried to question her.

The paramedic closest to him grabbed a clipboard and started taking information, which he wrote down and would no doubt give to the police. "What's your name?"

"Remigio Goyo."

His eyes widened. "Don Remigio Goyo?"

"Sí."

"I know your address. Soleado Goyo Estate, Castile-La Mancha. Are you acquainted with this woman?"

"No."

"Did you see the accident?"

"Sí," Remi said through gritted teeth. "We both tried to avoid an animal crossing the road at the same time. To her credit, her expertise at the wheel prevented a head-on collision."

"Did she tell you her name?"

"Jillian Gray. I'm not sure about the spelling of either name."

"Next of kin?"

"I don't know. The police will find out."

"She's very beautiful. Such hair…like spun gold."

Remi had been trying hard not to think about that, or the exquisite mold of her lovely body wearing a simple blouse and skirt. Drops of blood stood out against the pastel green material, staining what looked so perfect. That was the problem with great beauty. It hid the greatest flaws. Never again would he allow it to blind him.

"She's American. No doubt a tourist," Remi muttered, "but that's all I know. Did you find any other injuries besides the one to her eye?"

The paramedic shook his head. "No, but she's going to need surgery to remove whatever's lodged in there."

Remi's mind raced ahead. "Who's the best ophthamologist around?"

"Dr. Ernesto Filartigua from Madrid. He operates at the Hospital of the Holy Cross."

"Then tell the pilot to fly us there. I'll get the doctor on the phone. I want an expert on her case."

"Our company doesn't normally fly north of Toledo, but for you we will." Madrid was only a half hour farther than Toledo by car—not a great distance—and it meant getting her the best care.

Remi exhaled a deep breath. For once he was glad his title could make a difference. This time his judgment wasn't impaired. A life was in jeopardy, possibly because of him. He had no desire to take on another demon.

"Sign here, and I'll tell him to inform dispatch."

Remi put his signature to the dotted line. While the other man spoke to the cockpit, he pulled out his phone once more and asked for information. If it was at all possible, he wanted to speak to the doctor before they landed.

When he got through to the receptionist, he learned the doctor was in surgery. She would inform him an accident victim with an eye injury was being flown in. The E.R. would notify the doctor of her arrival.

A half hour later the helicopter landed on the helipad located at the east entrance of the hospital. They rushed her into the E.R., where Remi admitted her, promising to give the triage nurse more information when he heard from his foreman.

While he waited in the reception area, several different E.R. doctors went in the cubicle to examine her. A little later a moustached doctor in scrubs appeared. One of the staff showed him behind the curtain at the far end of the room.

Remi walked over to wait. When the doctor came out a few minutes later, he said, "Dr. Filartigua?"

"Sí?"

"I'm Remigio Goyo, the person who phoned for you to attend Senora Gray."

"Lucky for her you didn't waste any time, Don Remigio."

"How bad is her injury? I saw the accident. She said she couldn't see anything."

"That's common with a rupture like this. A glass shard has penetrated the globe of her right eye. The lab is running tests now to prepare her for surgery. After I get in there and remove it, I'll know more. Does she have family here?"

"No. I'm still trying to get answers from the police. Where can I wait while you're operating?"

"There's a reception area on the sixth floor, east wing."

"I'll be there." Tight bands constricted his breathing. "I've heard you're the best. Do whatever you have to."

His eyes studied Remi for a brief moment. "Of course."

"May I go in with her now?"

"If you wish, but it's not necessary. She's asleep. My advice to you is get a cup of coffee in the cafeteria." As he started to walk off he added, "You look like you could use one."

The doctor's comment reminded Remi he'd awakened with

no appetite and had turned down lunch during his business meeting with Luis.

Without conscious thought he walked over to the edge of the curtain. He wanted one last look at her before she went to surgery. The male lab technician darted him a glance, but Remi's gaze was drawn to her porcelainlike skin where the blood had been cleaned off. In a hospital gown, with her hair pulled back and covered, the pure lines of her classic facial features were even more pronounced.

In his mind's eye he could see her car rolling onto its side. He shuddered to think the result of that split-second moment might have done serious damage. If he'd been driving slower he probably would have applied the brakes, giving the other woman more room to maneuver. But all the ifs in the world wouldn't change what had happened.

More than ever he needed that coffee, so he left for the cafeteria. En route his cell rang. It was Paco. "We're back at the estate now. The police sent for a tow truck to haul the woman's car. You're supposed to phone Captain Perez in Toledo, Remi."

"Bueno." After writing down the number, he thanked Paco, then made the call to the investigating officer to let him know the woman in the accident was undergoing surgery in Madrid as they spoke. Remi answered his questions, then was told he could collect her purse and suitcase at police headquarters in Toldeo.

The officer could shed little light except that the twenty-seven-year-old American woman was driving a rental car from Lisbon, Portugal. EuropaUltimate Tours was payingfor it.

Remi pursed his lips. Did that mean she worked in Europe?

The police assumed they were her employer. They had put in a call to the tour company's personnel office in New York, but hadn't heard back yet.

He thanked the other man for the information and told him he'd be in touch. Without hesitation he called his distributor in New York, a man the Goyo family had worked with for years. He asked him to send one of his staff over to EuropaUltimate Tours and get the head of personnel to phone Remi back on his cell. It was an emergency.

While he waited, he ate a meal in the cafeteria. During his second cup of coffee, his phone rang. Within two minutes he'd explained the situation to the personnel department and was given the name and phone number of David Bowen, Jillian Gray's brother, who lived in Albany, New York.

Armed with that information, he hurried through the hospital and took the elevator to the sixth floor. The clerk at the nurse's station told him Senora Gray was still in surgery. He thanked the man before going to the reception area.

With no one there he could speak freely as he pulled out his phone and called the Senora's brother. The man answered on the fourth ring.

"Mr. Bowen?" he said in English. "My name's Remi Goyo. I'm calling from Holy Cross Hospital in Madrid, Spain. Before anything more is said, let me assure you your sister Jillian is all right, but she was in a car accident outside Toledo a few hours ago."

The other man groaned.

"I was the only person who witnessed it, that's why I'm calling. A piece of glass got in her eye."

"Dear Lord—"

"Dr. Filartigua, a revered eye surgeon in Madrid, is operating on her now. I knew you would want to be told."

"Thank you. I can't believe this has happened—not after what she's been through." The man sounded tormented.

Remi's hand tightened on the phone. "Is there something the doctor should know?"

"Her husband was killed in a car-truck accident in New York City a year ago. I begged her to stay with us for a while, but like a soldier she went right back to her work as a tour guide. It's an exhausting business. To be on her own yesterday means she must have taken the day off for a change. Her way of dealing with her grief I suppose."

Remi understood that need well enough.

"She's been trying to function ever since. For this to happen now…" His voice broke.

After hearing of her loss, Remi knew Jillian Gray would want her brother at her side no matter what. "How soon can you get here? I'll pick you up and bring you to the hospital."

"That's the problem. My wife is expecting our third baby in a month, but the pregnancy hasn't gone well. She has toxemia. If it gets any worse the doctor will have to deliver the baby early. I'm afraid to leave her in case something goes wrong in the delivery room, but I don't want Jilly to know the reason why. My sister thinks everything's fine."

A vein throbbed in Remi's temple. "I understand."

"We've kept my wife's condition a secret so Jilly wouldn't worry. She'd hoped to get pregnant herself, but there wasn't enough time before Kyle died. If she thought my wife was in trouble…I don't know what to do. She can't hear about it, not at a time like this. It would be too much for her. Has she called for me?"

He cleared his throat. "Not yet."

"I know Jilly needs me, but she'll hide it because that's the way she's made."

Remi had witnessed her bravery. When he'd asked her if she had family here, she'd said no and didn't expand on it.

Both brother and sister were determined to shield each other from the worst.

What a situation! In frustration his fingers made furrows through his hair. "I plan to see your sister through this. I won't leave her side."

"I can't ask you to do that—"

"I'm offering. The accident was partially my fault." Without preamble Remi explained exactly what had happened.

"It wasn't your fault," the other man confessed. "I wouldn't have stopped for an animal either. At that speed it's too dangerous. I'm just thankful you weren't hurt, too. What would she have done without your help?"

"Someone else would have come along."

"No one like you. Thank you, Mr. Goyo. Will you do me one more favor and let me know the second she's out of surgery? I don't care what time it is. When she's awake I want to speak to her. In the meantime I'm going to talk to my wife and the doctor. Depending on his advice, it's possible I could fly over for a quick trip."

"Don't worry about that right now. You take care of your wife, and I'll take care of your sister."

"I don't know how to repay you for this, but I'll think of something. Let me have your phone number."

After giving it to him he said, "You'd do the same for me, *verdad*?"

"Yes."

The man sounded so sincere Remi believed him. "Then say no more. We'll speak later."

Too restless to sit, Remi put the phone in his pocket and walked down the hall toward the nursing station. Maybe they knew something. Before he reached it he saw Dr. Filartigua coming out of the double doors of the surgery.

Remi walked over to him. "How bad was her injury?"

He pulled his mask down. "Bad."

The one-syllable answer hit him like a blow to the gut. "Bad enough to take away her vision?"

"Only time will tell. The glass splinter penetrated to the inner part of the globe. I removed it, but there'd been some internal bleeding. Surgically speaking, everything went well. The rest is up to nature. She appears to be in excellent health otherwise."

Remi was grateful for that much good news. "How soon can she leave the hospital?"

"She's in the recovery room now. If all goes well, they'll move her to a private room within the hour. Pending no other problems, I could release her by tomorrow afternoon. However, I suggest she stay an extra day to recover from the trauma of being in the accident. Have you been able to contact her family yet?"

"Yes, but her brother lives in New York and there's a problem."

The doctor listened. "Under the circumstances it's a good thing you're here to lend support. I'll want to see her in a week at my office. Then we'll know more about her ability to see. The nursing staff will send her home with instructions. She has to put drops in her eye three times a day for the first three days."

"Is she going to be in a lot of pain?"

"No, but within twenty-four hours she'll complain of it irritating her, and she'll want to rub it. Right now she has a small, cuplike patch taped over her eye to protect it day and night. Each time she needs the drops, she'll have to unfasten it. Otherwise, she can do normal activity, even read or watch television."

"What if she wants to go back to work?"

"Not for a month. The one thing I warn is that she doesn't bend over so her head is lower than her heart. When she's awake, you can tell her the operation was a success."

Their eyes met in silent understanding of what he didn't say.

"You have my number. If there's an emergency, my service will get in touch with me."

"Thank you, Doctor."

The second he left, Remi went back to the reception area to phone David Bowen. He wasn't going to like what Remi had to tell him.

Jillian heard voices before she came fully awake. She knew she was in a hospital. During the night a nurse had told her the operation was over and everything was fine. They were taking her to a private room. She'd had no idea what time that was.

When she finally opened her eyes, sunlight filtered in the room through the blinds. She couldn't see out of her right eye. Raising her hand to feel it, her fingers met with something plastic that had been firmly taped down.

A man's calloused hand caught hold of hers in a gentle grip. "Don't touch it, Jillian."

That deep voice—

She remembered his thickly accented English. He was the man at the accident scene.

Slowly turning her head she took in the tall, powerful-looking Spanish male standing at her side. Her hand was swallowed in his strong, warm grip. Until now she'd never realized how white her skin must look to a man whose natural olive complexion had been burnished by years in the sun.

Vibrant black hair was swept back from a widow's peak, highlighting hard, chiseled features. A true man of Castile. With those eyes, dark and brooding beneath equally black brows, she was put in mind of a figure from an El Greco painting.

Wearing a white shirt with the sleeves pushed up to the elbows, his pronounced five o'clock shadow lent him an earthy sensuality that took her by surprise. It had to be the anesthetic still in her system playing tricks with her mind.

"Are you my guardian angel?"

"If I were, you would never have had that accident." He gave her hand a small squeeze before relinquishing it.

"You were the driver of the other car?"

"Sí. I'm Remi."

The memory of their near miss flashed through her mind. "I—I could have killed you." She half moaned the words.

"It wouldn't have come to that. In any case, you were such an excellent driver, you turned aside in time."

She bit her lip. "I remember swerving and the sound of the helicopter, but little else."

"You're at the Holy Cross Hospital in Madrid."

"Madrid? I thought I was in Toledo."

"I had them fly you here so Dr. Filartigua could operate. He's an expert eye surgeon."

She tried to swallow but her mouth was too dry. "Thank you. The nurse told me the operation was a success."

He studied her intently. "The doctor told me the same thing. Would you like some juice? Then we'll get your brother on the phone. He's anxious to talk to you."

She let out a small cry of surprise. "How did David find out about this?"

"I made inquiries through your work. When I told them what happened, they said to tell you not to worry about anything. All they cared about was your getting better. They gave me your brother's name and phone number so I could get hold of him."

"I see."

He handed her a paper cup from her breakfast tray. The chilled apple juice tasted good. She drank all of it and handed the empty container back to him. *"Gracias, Senor."*

"De nada, Senora."

She had a feeling he was laughing at her. "I know my Spanish needs a lot of work."

"You made yourself perfectly clear at the accident scene. I was impressed. If I sounded amused just now, it's because you seem totally recovered from your operation. I wasn't expecting it quite this fast."

Even if he was lying about her Spanish, she was glad to feel this good already. She raised the head of the bed with the remote so she could sit up. That's when she saw an arrangement of yellow and white roses interspersed with daisies placed on the table.

"Did you bring me those beautiful flowers?"

"Sí, Senora."

"They're gorgeous! Would you move the table closer so I can smell them?"

"I'll do better than that." He picked up the vase and carried it over to her. She buried her nose in one of the roses.

"They smell so sweet."

"I'm glad you like them."

"Who wouldn't?" she cried softly. "Thank you!"

After he'd put them back, she spotted an unmade cot in front of the closet door. Her gaze darted to his. "You *slept* with me?"

His lips twitched. "Guilty as charged." The man's masculine charisma was lethal.

Her words had come out the wrong way. Heat rushed to her face like a swarm of bees. "What about your family waiting at home for you?"

A subtle change in his expression hardened his features. "What family would that be?" His acerbic question stopped her cold. "No doubt my staff was delighted by my absence," he added in a mocking voice, but she saw no levity in his piercing black eyes.

"Why would you stay here with me?"

He stood there with his legs slightly apart, his hands on his hips. She'd never known a man so ultimately male. "I promised your brother I'd look after you. Would you like to call him now, or after you've eaten your breakfast?"

"I'd better phone him first. He took care of me after our parents died. Even after I was married he never got over the habit."

"He told me you lost your husband a year ago. I'm sorry. Naturally he's concerned."

Jillian wished her brother hadn't said anything. She sucked in her breath. "He worries too much about me."

He cocked his head. "Where his sister is concerned, that's a brother's prerogative surely?"

"Do you have sisters?"

"No." In an instant his eyes darkened, making her wish she hadn't said anything. "Use my phone." He handed her his cell. "I programmed his number. Press eight."

As she took the phone from him, their fingers brushed. His touch sent little trickles of awareness up her arm.

He was a take-charge kind of male with a daunting, innate authority others wouldn't dare to challenge. In Jillian's case he'd left nothing to chance. Because of him she'd been given the finest care possible in the shortest amount of time. If that wasn't enough, he'd watched over her all night.

She owed him a great deal, possibly her life. By the time her brother answered the phone, she was feeling rather emotional.

"Dave?"

"Thank heaven, Jilly. How are you feeling?"

"I'm fine. How are Angela and the children?"

"They're great. You sound too well for someone who's just survived an accident and an operation."

"The seat belt kept me from being hurt, and the Senor was right there to get me to the hospital. It's just my eye. I've been told the operation went without problem." She fought to keep the wobble out of her voice.

"Are you in bad pain?"

"No. Not at all."

"Don't lie to me."

"I'm not." That horrific pain had gone.

"Let me speak to Senor Goyo."

"Goyo?"

"I don't think you're fully awake yet, Jilly. Remi Goyo's the man who's been taking care of you."

She almost dropped the phone. Her gaze darted to the window where he stood looking out through the slats, his expression remote.

Before the accident she'd stopped in front of the gate at the Soleado Goyo estate to speak to the owner, but one of the workers told her Don Remigio had gone to Toledo on business. She would have better luck if she called him first.

Don was a word used for a titled person in Spain. Now that she thought about it she remembered seeing a coat of arms emblazoned in the tile work of the arched gate.

"Senor Goyo?" At the sound of her voice, he turned in her direction. "Are you Don Remigio?"

"Sí?"

He moved toward her. "My name's Remi," he reminded her in a low tone before reaching for the phone.

Yes, she knew that, but having learned he was an aristo-
crat, it put everything on a slightly different footing. Again
she felt the warmth of his fingers and trembled as he took his
cell from her. It *had* to be the operation making her senses
come alive to him. Since Kyle's death she hadn't looked at
another man. She couldn't.

Her husband had been an attractive, russet-haired guy with
warm brown eyes she'd met working for EuropaUltimate
Tours. Three inches taller than her five-foot-six frame, they'd
been a perfect fit in every way and had married within six
months. They'd been so happy, she'd never imagined the day
coming when it would all end without warning.

That's the way *her* accident had happened. One minute she
was driving along the highway, excited by her latest idea for a
new tour. The next minute a stranger was carrying her from the
wreck, urging her not to touch her injured eye. He was a man
with supreme confidence who knew exactly what to do and had
managed to keep her fear from escalating out of control.

CHAPTER TWO

JILLIAN STRAINED to hear his side of the conversation with her brother, but it was difficult because he'd turned his back toward her. Maybe the action was unintentional, but it frustrated her, particularly since she was helplessly drawn to the play of muscle across his broad shoulders.

There she went again noticing everything about this remarkable stranger who lit his own fires in a crisis while others just stood around reeling in confusion. No one else could have summoned a helicopter that fast.

The nurse chose that moment to come in and take her vital signs. Before the other woman left the room, she moved the rolling table forward so Jillian could eat her breakfast.

Halfway through her breakfast Remi walked over and handed her back the phone. "Your brother wants to say goodbye."

What had they been talking about for such a long time? She lifted the phone to her ear. "Hey, thanks for remembering you wanted to talk to me," she teased.

"Remi told me you were being examined. Naturally I wanted to thank him for everything he's done for you. I'm trying to make arrangements to fly over."

"Don't come, Dave. I'll be flying back to New York as

soon as I'm discharged. Luckily I'm in Madrid, where I'm already ticketed."

"How can you leave? Remi told me the doctor expects to see you back in his office in a week."

She flashed a covert glance to the arresting male standing next to her bed. He seemed to know a lot more about her situation than she did.

"That's not a problem, Dave. I'll go to an eye surgeon in New York for a checkup. Right now I've got work to do. I'll slip up to Albany in a couple of weeks."

"Let me talk to Remi again, Jilly."

No way. She loved her overprotective brother, but he went too far. She felt guilty enough the owner of Soleado Goyo had felt compelled to spend the night with her. Kyle had told her she snored. How embarrassing.

"Tell the children I bought some souvenirs I know they'll love, and I found the most beautiful christening outfit for the baby in Coimbra. I picked up something for you, too, but it's a surprise. See you soon. Love you."

On that note she pressed the disconnect button and handed the phone to the man whose black gaze flickered over her without letting her know what he was thinking.

She pinned him with her good eye. His dark vital presence stood out against the sterile background of her room. "When did you speak to the doctor?"

"Right after your surgery."

"I'd like to talk to him about getting out of here."

"You just woke up."

Jillian drew in a deep breath. "I feel good. It isn't as if I was knocked unconscious or anything. Thanks to you the best surgeon has operated on my eye. I'm not even in pain.

I'll go crazy if I just have to lie here. If you were in my shoes, you wouldn't stand for it, either."

The furrow between those black brows deepened. "How do you know that?"

"Because the second you're not busy you start pacing around."

His eyes mirrored a faint respect for her observation.

"I recognize the signs, Senor, believe me. The fact is I'm made the same way you are. No doubt you're dying to get back to your olive groves, but your sense of responsibility to me has kept you here. I'm sorry for that."

He put a hand behind his neck and rubbed it absently. "Who told you the nature of my business?"

"No one. When Dave said your last name was Goyo, I realized you had to be the owner of Soleado Goyo." *And a very important person.*

She knew she'd caught his interest by the way he shifted his weight. "You're familiar with the brand?"

"I've cooked with your olive oil many times. In my opinion it's unmatched. While I was driving past all those olive groves yesterday, I slowed down to ask a worker about them."

"No one told me."

"I don't know why they would. I—"

But before she could finish her explanation, a man in a moustache and a blue summer suit walked in the room. He nodded to Senor Goyo. "Good morning, Senora Gray. I'm Dr. Filartigua."

She breathed a sigh of relief. "I've been hoping you would come in. Thank you for operating on me. I know I'm very lucky."

"That's my job. How are you feeling?"

"Well enough to leave."

"I'm gratified to hear it, but I insist you stay an extra day to give your body a chance to get over the shock of the accident."

"I feel fine, Doctor. I need to get back to my job in New York right away."

He shook his head. "No flying for a month."

"A month—"

"The air pressure changes on a jet could cause problems. You want to heal as quickly as possible, don't you?"

She fought not to cry out her disappointment. "Of course."

"You can do normal activities, but no driving on your own. I'll take a look at your eye in a week and we'll see what's going on in there."

His comment jarred her. "But it was just a piece of glass. I thought the operation was successful."

"Indeed it was, but only time will tell us how much permanent damage was done internally."

Her body shuddered in reaction. "Are you saying my sight could be impaired?"

"It's possible, but concentrate on getting well and letting nature take its course. The nurse will be coming in to start you on a course of drops for the next three days. They'll stem any infection. Enjoy being pampered. Everyone needs it once in a while."

"But—"

"No arguing." He smiled. "I'll check on you again in the morning. If all is well, then you'll be released." He patted her arm and left the room.

A familiar male hand grasped hers. She tried to pull away but he held on. Jillian knew what he was trying to do, but if he dared say one word, she feared she would howl the place down.

Blind? Or close to it in one eye? She couldn't comprehend it.

Her thoughts turned to her late husband, who hadn't

been given any odds. He'd died on impact with that semi. How did she dare complain when she still had the sight out of her left eye?

After surviving the precarious moment, she eased her hand from Senor Goyo's firm grip. "I'm all right," she whispered.

"In that case I'm going to drive to Toledo for your purse and suitcase. I presume you travel with a laptop."

He understood a lot. She nodded without looking at him.

"You can work from your hospital bed. I won't be long." As he started to leave she called to him.

"Don Remigio—"

He paused in the doorway. "I answer to Remi," he said, his voice grating.

The last thing she wanted to do was offend him. "Remi, then. I'm so indebted to you, I don't know where to start."

"That's good. It helps assuage my guilt."

"The accident was my fault, not yours."

"You're entitled to your opinion. Mind the nurse while I'm gone." He disappeared.

The room seemed bigger without his virile presence.

And much emptier, she realized after he'd been gone a few minutes. Since the rollover he'd been her constant companion, waking or sleeping.

She should be glad he'd gone. Tomorrow she would take a taxi to the Prado Inn, where she'd intended to stay before catching her flight. For the next week she would do what she could on the computer.

By using a taxi to get around, she could take time out to look for some different and interesting spots in Madrid's environs to add to the new itinerary.

In the middle of making plans, the nurse came in to put three sets of drops in her eye. When she lifted the patch,

Jillian couldn't see anything, but the nurse told her that was normal this soon after surgery.

Yes, it was normal if you were blind....

As the other woman was refastening the tape, the phone rang at the side of her bed. The nurse picked up the receiver and handed it to her before leaving the room.

Only Jillian's brother knew to reach her here at the hospital. She spoke into the phone. "David Bowen, if you're checking on me again, I'll have you know I'm fine!"

"You sound in a bit of a temper," came Remi's heavily accented voice. The sound of it caused her heart to turn over for no good reason. "You must be getting better."

Heat crept into her face. "I'm sorry you got the brunt of that outburst. It's just that I don't like my brother worrying about me when they've got a baby on the way."

"He told me."

Good heavens. The two men sounded like they'd been friends for years.

"As for the reason I'm calling, I thought I'd ask if you need any shopping done."

She blinked. "That's very kind of you, but everything I require is in my suitcase or my purse."

"*Muy bien*. Then I'll see you within three hours." He clicked off.

Jillian hung up the phone thinking he was more protective than Dave, and that was really saying something. For some reason Senor Goyo felt a sense of responsibility toward her she didn't want or deserve. Too bad he'd overheard what the doctor had said.

She hated it when people felt sorry for her. After Kyle's death she couldn't get back to work fast enough. The people on the tour buses didn't know anything about her or her life. That's the way she liked to keep it.

"*Buenos dias, Senora*." A custodian had entered the room and hurriedly made up the cot Remi had slept in. She folded it against the closet doors. It reminded Jillian she didn't want him sleeping in here with her again tonight.

The woman emptied the wastebasket, then swept the room before leaving again. No sooner was Jillian alone than the nurse came in to get her up so she could go to the bathroom. On her own she washed her hands and face, then brushed her teeth with the necessities provided. Afterward she felt good enough to take a little walk around the room.

When she climbed into bed the nurse took her vital signs, gave her a smile and turned on the TV for her. "Once Senor Goyo has returned with your things, I'll help you shower."

"That would be wonderful. Blood got in my hair."

"Until your appointment with Dr. Filartigua, you won't be able to wash it with water. We have a dry shampoo here you apply and then brush out."

After the nurse left, someone else brought her another apple juice. Jillian had never had such service. It was because of the Senor. Talk about pampering. Yet all the attention in the world wouldn't stop her mind from thinking about her injury.

Could you get a driver's license if you could only see out of one eye? Jillian thought so, but she would check.

She had to be able to drive to do her job, and she needed *that* job. It kept her so busy she didn't have time to dwell on Kyle's accident or the death of their dreams to get pregnant and eventually own their own tour company.

They'd planned to have it all. Instead they'd only been allowed eighteen months of marriage before tragedy struck.

Even with her patch on, tears rolled down both cheeks. Great…

Jillian could hear Senor Goyo telling her not to cry so the tears wouldn't irritate her injury. What difference did it make now?

She reached for some tissues on the bedside table to mop up, realizing she was wallowing in self-pity. What a disaster she'd turned out to be. The second she had her laptop back, she'd look up the rules for a New York driver's license and find out what she could or couldn't do with one eye.

Remi stepped out of the main police station in Toledo. He waved to Paco, who'd brought Remi's car from home. Diego nodded to him as he pulled up behind the foreman in one of the estate cars. Both men walked over to him.

"Thanks for coming." He put Jillian's purse and suitcase in the backseat, where he could see the overnight bag he'd asked Maria to pack for him.

Paco changed places with him and shut the door. "When will you be back?"

"Tomorrow." He'd already instructed Maria to prepare his parents' room for her on the main floor. No one had slept there since his widowed mother had passed away. He had an idea Jillian would enjoy it. "Senora Gray will be staying with us for at least a month. She can't fly to the States before then and she has no family here."

He'd just gotten off the phone with David Bowen, who had too much on his plate worrying about his pregnant wife to consider leaving her. Jillian's brother couldn't thank him enough for helping out at a time like this and insisted on transferring some funds to his account. Remi told him to forget it.

"What did the doctor say about her eye?"

A tight band constricted Remi's lungs. "Barring a miracle I'm afraid there'll be permanent damage. It's a matter of how much."

"That's a tragedy."

Diego frowned. "I wonder if she could possibly be the American who stopped at the entrance to the estate right before the accident happened."

It had to be Jillian. She'd mentioned talking to one of the workers. "Was she blond?"

"Like liquid gold." Diego made a gesture with his hand, the kind that meant the woman's looks could strike a man dumb. "She wanted to talk to the owner. I told her to call you."

He lowered his head. She wouldn't have to do that now, but the fact that she hadn't brought it up yet led him to believe she didn't plan to. He gritted his teeth.

"I've got to get going." Remi looked at Paco. "Call me if an emergency comes up."

"Por supuesto."

After thanking both men, he took off for Madrid wondering what her visit to the estate yesterday had been all about. Before long he'd have answers, but right now he intended to stay within the speed limit. It would be a long time, if ever, before he could shake off yesterday's trauma.

Once back in Madrid he checked in at a hotel near the hospital to shower and shave. A change of shirt and trousers made him feel more human. When he glanced at his watch, he realized she would have eaten her lunch a long time ago. He'd buy something for himself in the cafeteria and take it up to her room to eat while she worked.

The police wanted to talk to her, but he'd put them off by telling them about her eye injury. At that point they agreed to wait until she was settled at the estate.

Everything had been decided, except that she hadn't been

let in on Remi's plans yet. In his gut he knew she'd say no, but he was already prepared for her response. If there was one thing he was good at, it was negotiation—an art that had pulled the family business on solid footing again no thanks to his brother.

Two years ago all had looked hopeless, but something inside hadn't let him give up. If he had anything to say about it, he wouldn't let her give up, either, no matter the prognosis.

Forty-five minutes later he entered her hospital room to find her bed empty. Either she was in the bathroom, or down the hall getting some exercise.

Three more flower arrangements guaranteed to cheer her up had been wheeled into the room on a small cart; one of pink carnations, the other two a mix of wildflowers. Any more furniture in the room would make it impossible for the nursing staff to maneuver.

He lowered the suitcase to the floor next to the wall. After putting her purse on the side table, he sat down in the only chair and began munching on his steak sandwich while he waited for her to appear.

A few more seconds and the bathroom door opened. When she saw him, she let out a squeal and held the back of her gown together, the epitome of the modest female.

He struggled not to smile. "I've closed my eyes. Let me know when I can open them again."

Her bare feet made a padding sound as she hurried past him. He heard the sound of her raising the head of the bed with the remote. Then came the rustle of the sheet. "You can look now."

When he dared, he noticed she'd already reached for her purse and was brushing her hair. It splayed about her neck and shoulders in a silky swirl.

"Thank you for bringing me my things. Throughout this

whole experience you've gone way beyond the call of duty and I'll be eternally grateful. But now that I have my belongings back, I want you to leave. If you try to do anything more for me, then I'll start to feel uncomfortable."

He'd known what she was going to say before she said it, so he deliberately finished off the rest of his sandwich before speaking again.

"I thought you wanted your laptop. If you'll allow me, I'll open your suitcase and set it up for you."

She shook her head. "I'll do it."

"The doctor cautioned you're not supposed to bend over yet. The sudden blood flow to your head might disturb your wound."

"I—I didn't know that," she stammered. "He should have instructed *me*."

"He assumed I would tell you."

After a moment she said, "When the nurse comes in again, I'll ask her to do it."

Remi could only see her one eye. Between darkly fringed lashes it shimmered a green hue like new shoots of spring grass. Combined with the gleam of her golden hair, he discovered her coloring was like the velvety gold liquid with its glints of green found in a prized bottle of Goyo's extra fine virgin olive oil—one of the most beautiful sights in the world to him when held up to the light.

He lifted a dark brow. "Why bother her with a nonmedical request when she's been run off her feet bringing you flowers from all your admirers."

She fidgeted with the sheet. "They're from my brother and the people at work."

"I'm sure you're sorely missed." He rose to his feet. "Since I'm here, why not let me help?"

She looked away quickly. "All right," she said in a tentative voice. "Thank you, but then you have to go."

Remi let that comment pass and reached for her suitcase. He put it on the chair. "What's the code on the lock?"

"K F G."

Her husband's initials?

He opened it with no problem. Beneath the padding of several layers of filmy lingerie he found her laptop nestled among her clothes. The adaptor was already attached to the cord. All he had to do was insert it in the Internet outlet on the wall behind her bed.

"There you are." He placed it on her lap, inadvertently brushing her arm in the process. The touch of her soft, smooth skin shouldn't have fazed him, but to his chagrin he felt her warmth long after he'd straightened away from her bed. That hadn't happened for several years. He hadn't thought it possible to respond to a woman's touch ever again.

Out of the periphery he watched for her to lift the lid, but she made no such move. Clearly she wanted him out of her room and her life, but he had no intention of going anywhere.

Instead he pulled his cell phone from his pocket and called Fermin, who ran the bottling plant on the estate. Today the weekly shipment to England needed to be loaded onto the trucks. Remi normally checked every case that went out, but today Fermin would have to be relied on to do it without him.

In order to start making a profit, Remi had long ago pared down the staff to the hardest workers who remained loyal to him. Judging by Luis's figures, Remi's efforts had paid off and everything was going well, even better than expected.

After planting himself in the chair, which he purposely turned the other way to avoid the frustrated looks Senora Gray kept sending him, he immersed himself in conversation with the older man who knew the business like the inside of his pocket. They discussed rehiring Jorge Diaz.

The younger man had been wanting to come back to Goyo's on a permanent basis for some time now. Remi conceded that Jorge had always been a good worker, even if he'd been caught between conflicting loyalties for a time. When he and Fermin finally concluded business, Remi promised he'd think about it.

On a final note he told Fermin he would find a sizable bonus in his next paycheck for sticking with him over the last two difficult years. It would be the first of many such installments for his unfailing devotion to Remi and the business.

The older man got all choked up before they said goodbye.

Without pausing for breath Remi phoned the company that had done the wiring for the Internet on the estate. He wanted someone sent out as soon as possible to put an outlet in the master bedroom of the main house.

When an arrangement was made for the next day, a pleased Remi thanked the man before phoning Maria to tell her about it. He was curious to know how things were shaping up at the main house. She assured him their guest would want for nothing. While she commiserated over the Senora's eye injury, the nurse came in the room to put in more drops and take her vital signs.

Remi walked out to the hall to give them privacy.

As long as he still had Maria on the line, he cautioned her against saying anything about the injury to Senora Gray. The American woman didn't like being reminded of it. The less said, the better. Maria assured him she'd be the soul of discretion.

Once he'd rung off, he saw orderlies down the hall bringing dinners from the kitchen. Surprised at the lateness of the hour, he realized the day had gotten away from him without his being aware of it. Before one of the men could enter Jillian's room, Remi said he'd take it in to her.

Pulling some bills from his wallet he asked if another dinner could be sent up for him. One small sandwich hadn't been enough. He was still hungry.

The younger man refused the money, but told Remi to wait and he'd be right back with another dinner for him.

Excellent.

Remi stood outside the door enjoying the idea of fencing with her—that age-old Castilian dance usually involving two men at home with a sword made of the hardest Toledo steel.

Though she wielded her own feminine weapon very well and knew some fancy footwork that made her a worthy opponent, she'd never come up against a Goyo before. Senora Gray was about to be taught some moves still unknown to her.

Once the nurse had gone, Jillian sent a few e-mails to her boss, Pia, and a few coworkers thanking them for the flowers, but for some odd reason she didn't feel like digging in to real work after all. At the moment she wasn't capable of much more than twiddling her thumbs.

It appeared Senor Goyo had decided to obey her request and leave the hospital. She'd hoped he would go, but now that she was alone, she had to admit she missed his electrifying presence, the only words to describe his effect on her.

The degree of the Spaniard's male beauty was off the charts and she'd only been taking in his striking attributes out of *one* eye. What would happen if she could see him full vision?

Place a suit of armor made from the finest Toledo steel on his hard-muscled body and he could be one of those incredible-looking conquistadors sweeping across the New World with Cortez. Come to think of it, didn't the gorgeous Pedro in *Captain from Castile* go by the name "de Vargas"?' One of Senor Goyo's ancestors perhaps?

She was being foolish with all her fantasies, but deep down she recognized this important man was someone unforgettable. A man in his thirties was normally married with children. Jillian would love to know his history, but she'd caught a glimpse of his dark side earlier and didn't feel brave enough to trespass. She didn't have the right, not when she owed him so much.

Restless, she turned on her side, careful not to let the laptop slip to the floor. The last thing she needed was time on her hands. It made her think, and when she started to think, she began to feel sorry for herself. That would never do.

She turned on her back again and opened the laptop to play solitaire. She hadn't been driven to do this for a long time. While she tested herself to see how fast she could move the aces and kings into position, the door opened.

When she looked up, her breath caught to see the object of her musings walk inside. He'd come bearing more gifts. The aroma of roast beef permeated the hospital room. She'd thought she wasn't hungry, but his stimulating presence piqued her appetite.

Earlier she'd noticed that he'd found time to shower and shave. A navy sports shirt and white khakis molded his powerful chest and thighs. She decided she liked him better in modern clothing. Silver armor would have covered up that well-defined physique.

There she went again marveling over his considerable male charms. Secretly excited he'd returned to her room, she was confused, *stunned* by her reaction to him.

Just last week she'd turned down yet another guy for dinner. One of her friends at work had warned her the day would come when she'd want to start living again. Jillian had shaken her head. She wasn't interested. No man would ever compare to Kyle.

But that was before she'd had the accident. When she'd least expected it, a stranger had come along to rescue her. She'd been whisked away to a hospital by a man from La Mancha.

Helpless to do otherwise, she stole another glance at him. That's when the realization hit.

No man could compare to the Senor, either.

The revelation shocked her into silence, but he took no notice. After removing her laptop he rolled the table across her body. "Your dinner, Senora." He lifted the cover off the dinner plate. "I believe it's edible."

Without looking at him she muttered, "You mean you're not sure?"

"Are you asking me to test it first?" he countered. "I had no idea that inside your deceptive shell beats the heart of Cleopatra."

Until she'd sensed an edge to his tone, she'd thought he was being playful.

What an odd thing to say. In what way did she look deceptive?

Without waiting for her answer he picked up one of the forks and ate a piece of her meat. After letting it digest he said, "It will do. However, we'll give it five minutes just to make sure."

"Don't be silly." She grabbed the other fork. After cutting herself a bite of roast beef, she quickly finished it off.

His black eyes glittered. "You live dangerously, don't you, Senora."

Jillian's coworkers had made comments of that nature before. When Kyle had first met her, he'd called her fearless. They'd all said it in a teasing manner, but coming from this man's lips made it feel like a criticism.

"Perhaps you say that because you see a lot of yourself in me, Senor," she ventured boldly.

Between dark lashes his eyes gleamed with a strange light. "Touché."

While he took his plate and sat down in the chair to eat, she felt caught up in emotions foreign to her experience up to now. It was frightening and exhilarating at the same time.

"Play a lot of solitaire, do you?" came the innocent sounding question.

She stopped munching on her roll. Nothing got past his all-seeing gaze. "I presume you turn to darts when you find yourself at a loose end."

He flashed her a wicked smile. "Knives are more my style."

"I was going to say that," she assured him without batting an eye, "but at the last second I chose not to presume in case I irritated your sensibilities."

A bark of laughter escaped his tanned throat. "I thought you decided I didn't have any."

"You have to have some, otherwise you wouldn't have been the angel who made it possible for me to recover this quickly. Which brings me to what I wanted to say earlier."

To her frustration he kept eating as if he had little interest in the conversation.

"I truly appreciate everything you've done for me, but I don't require your help any longer and would like to repay you."

"You sound like your brother."

Exasperated, she wiped her mouth with a napkin. "I mean it, Senor."

"Remi. That's the third time I've had to remind you."

She was very much aware of that fact, but calling him by his first name put them on a more intimate footing. After tonight Jillian didn't plan to see him again. Though she felt a sense of deprivation just thinking about it, she had to draw the line somewhere.

"I'm aware you won't let me give you money, so the only thing I can do is release you from your promise to my brother. The truth is, I'd like to be alone tonight and know you would, too."

In a lightning move he got up and put his empty plate on the tray. His enigmatic gaze sought hers. "For a woman I only met yesterday, you claim to know a great deal about me."

She took a deep breath. "I've eaten your olive oil. After seeing those groves I realize you're a man with great responsibilities, Remi."

"At last you say my name," he drawled with satisfaction.

Jillian averted her eyes. "I'd be a lot happier if you gave up the vigil and left me to my own devices. You're always on the phone and need to get on with your life. So do I," she finished, her voice throbbing.

"Surely not tonight."

She had no answer for that.

When he placed his bronzed hands on the edge of the table, she noted inconsequently there was no white wedding ring mark on his third finger. Had he ever worn one? The action brought him closer to her body. She caught the faint fragrance of the soap he'd used in the shower, creating more havoc with her senses.

"You look tired. Why don't we continue this conversation tomorrow before you're discharged? I presume there are other people anxious to receive an e-mail from you this evening. Since you pointed out I have many things to attend to," he mocked, "I'll say good-night now and see you after we've both had some sleep.

"If you need me for any reason, phone the Casa Cervantes

here in Madrid. It's not that far from the hospital. They'll put your call through to me. *Buenas noches,* Jillian."

On his way out the door he wheeled the cot into the hall with him, ostensibly to make more space in her room.

"Buenas noches," she whispered to his retreating back, experiencing more disappointment because he'd never had any intention of spending another night with her.

CHAPTER THREE

DR. FILARTIGUA refastened the tape. "You're coming along fine, Senora. The drops will help the irritation you're starting to feel, but it should only last a day or two. I'll sign the discharge papers and send the nurse to wheel you out to the exit. Do you have any questions for me?"

"Only one," she murmured quietly, "but I know I have to wait for the answer."

"You're being very brave. Keep it up and don't forget— my receptionist has put you down for eleven o'clock next Thursday in my office. It's on the ground floor of the building across from the main entrance to the hospital."

"I'll be there. Thank you for everything, Doctor."

He nodded. "The nurse will give you printed instructions with my phone number. Call me anytime if you have a problem." After patting her arm, he left the room.

Jillian was glad he'd made his rounds early so she could leave before the Senor made his appearance. Her bag was packed. She'd dressed in her favorite uncrushable yellow shirtwaist dress with the capped sleeves. With her eye and part of her face covered by tape, there was little point bothering with makeup except for lipstick.

While she waited for the nurse, she went in the bathroom

to brush her hair, leaving it to fall naturally in a side parting. The dry shampoo seemed to have done its job, but she missed the fragrance from her own strawberry-scented shampoo.

Much as she wanted to take all the flowers with her, it would be too much trouble to load and unload them at the hotel. She would keep the Senor's roses and leave the rest for patients in the hospital who would appreciate them the most.

"Oh—" she cried, almost colliding with Remi as she left the bathroom with her purse. He steadied her with both strong hands on her upper arms. His fiery black eyes swept over her with such intensity, she could hardly breathe.

"Apparently you're in a hurry to leave," he said in a deep, husky tone. "I don't blame you."

She felt the warmth of his breath on her lips. The sensation brought her close to a faint and she eased out of his hold. "I—I've been discharged," she explained, her voice faltering.

"I know."

Of course he did.

He'd come to her room looking incredibly appealing in a tan sport shirt and cream-colored chinos. Behind him she saw the nurse come in pushing a wheelchair. "Time to go, Senora Gray. Are you ready?"

"Yes, but I need to call for a taxi first."

"It's already been taken care of. Sit down, *por favor.*"

Jillian saw Remi put his booted foot behind one of the wheels so it wouldn't move on her. At this juncture she had no choice but to do the older woman's bidding.

"The flowers—"

"I'll load them," he said near her ear, sending a shockwave through her trembling body.

"Leave the flowers from my coworkers for the nurse to give to some other patients, will you please?"

"If that's your wish."

"It is."

The next thing she knew the nurse was wheeling her from the room. Like a dutiful new father, Remi followed with her suitcase in one hand and the flowers in his other arm, but there was no baby. She felt a fraud.

On their trip through the halls and down the elevator, every female in the hospital within their radius devoured Remi with her eyes. No matter what Jillian had to do, she made a mental note to squelch the urge to look at him in the same way.

A black sedan bearing the same crest she'd seen on the gate of the estate stood parked outside the automatic doors. It came as no surprise she had her own private taxi service offered by none other than the most outrageously attractive male on the planet.

Jillian could make that statement with the greatest of authority.

For the last six years she'd been around hundreds of striking men from almost every country who'd been on tours across Europe. Yet unlike the majority of them, Remi seemed oblivious to the interest he created among women and men alike.

She had a hunch he'd been born with other things on his mind than himself, a quality she rated right at the top of a man's most desirable qualities.

After he'd assisted her into the front passenger seat, the nurse handed her a sack containing her drops and a printout of instructions.

"Good luck, Senora. *Vaya con dios.*"

"*Gracias, Senora.*"

The woman shut the door. When Jillian turned her head, she watched Remi put the two bouquets on the floor of the backseat, then shut the door. After a chat with the nurse he joined Jillian in front, filling the atmosphere with his own intoxicating male scent mixed with the smell of leather.

As soon as he turned on the ignition she said, "I have reservations at the Prado Inn."

The powerful engine made a low purring sound. "Your room won't be ready until this afternoon."

"I know. I'm planning to work at a table in the bar of the hotel while I wait."

"Work is the great panacea, *verdad*?" The way he'd spoken let her know he was no stranger to it.

With a change of gear he drove out to the tree-lined street, maneuvering them through the heavy morning traffic with practiced ease. It already promised to be a hot, sunny day as they made their way to the other side of the colorful city without talking. Between the profusion of flowers and playing fountains, Madrid had a beauty all its own.

Strange that with only one eye to see through, every sense seemed to be enhanced. The sky looked bluer, food tasted better, the roses smelled sweeter, a man's deep voice penetrated to her insides, a man's touch sent her blood surging.

Jillian could thank the disturbing male at the wheel for this meteoric thrust back into the life she'd thought was over when Kyle never came home again.

Oh, darling…It should be you making me feel this way.

Before she realized it Remi pulled the car into the first empty parking space at the side of the street. After shutting off the motor he turned to her, his bronzed arm outstretched along the top of the seat. Leaning closer, he wiped the salty tears off her chin with his finger. "How can I help, Jillian?"

With those words she realized he thought she'd broken down because of her eye injury. The pathos in his tone moved her in ways she didn't know were possible. She sniffed and raised her head to look out at one of the many gardens bordering the sidewalks.

"You've done everything humanly possible. I'm very grateful," she said, her voice shaking.

"Grateful enough to tell me what's really going on inside?" His deep timbre resonated to her bones.

She struggled for composure. For her own emotional sanity it would be better never to see him again. Because he felt partially guilty for the accident, he'd been her Good Samaritan, but she had no reason to read any more into it.

It wasn't his fault he made her feel things she didn't want to feel, wasn't ready to feel. That's what was really going on.

Forcing a gentle laugh she said, "Don't mind me, Remi. Every so often I have a day or two where I get emotional for no particular reason."

His arm remained in place behind her, catching the ends of her hair.

"Is that why you were on your own day before yesterday?"

"Yes…" She grabbed at the first excuse he'd supplied.

"It wouldn't have been because you'd wanted to meet with me specifically?"

Her heart picked up speed. She jerked her head around to look at him, freeing those golden strands that had been pressed against his skin, with its smattering of black hairs. Being in such close proximity to him, she felt like every sense had been magnified to the hundredth power.

"Why would you ask that?"

"Because I questioned the worker you talked to. He happened to be Diego, one of my assistants."

Jillian clutched her purse in reaction. She might have known.

"He said you asked questions about the owner and he told you to call and make an appointment with me. When he told me what time you'd stopped to talk to him, I realized you couldn't have been on the road ten minutes before the accident."

"That's true," she whispered.

Silence ensued before he said, "Why did you want to see me? Obviously you had a particular reason in mind, otherwise you'd have been off somewhere on a tour bus for the day."

She lowered her head. He had her squirming. "I—I'm afraid I made a mistake."

At her remark, she felt his body tauten. "In what way?" he asked.

Afraid she'd offended him again, she moistened her lips nervously. "I wanted to discuss business with you, but since then I've changed my mind."

"You send mixed messages, Senora. Did you not tell me I was an angel with some redeeming qualities?"

Without an honest answer, he would never let this go. She stirred restlessly in the seat. "It's because you've already been so wonderful to me, I don't want you to feel I'm taking advantage of your good nature."

"I could hardly assume that when the accident happened *after* you'd made an effort to talk to me."

Defeated, she exhaled softly before saying, "All right. I've been a tour guide for EuropaUtimate Tours six years now. On occasion I help plan their itineraries. So far in France and Spain they've concentrated on the main tourist attractions along the French Riviera and the Costa del Sol. I'm trying to put a different trip together that includes the less-frequented parts of central Spain and Portugal."

His penetrating gaze played over her features. "Most tourists want a beach vacation."

"I agree, but then there are tourists like me who like to learn things and explore."

He stared at her through veiled eyes. "Somehow that doesn't surprise me."

She decided he found her amusing. Taking a fortifying breath she said, "Our tour buses make stops at all kinds of places, including vineyards, but we've never offered an olive grove as an educational part of a tour before.

"As I was driving along yesterday, I passed several miles of them and the idea came to me to speak to the owner. When I came to the gate I saw the words *Soleado Goyo* fashioned in the grillwork. The man told me the estate was owned by the *Conde*.

"Before the accident happened I was hoping you might consider allowing our tour buses to stop at your estate and enjoy a small tour of the olive groves. To my knowledge our company has never offered an excursion like that here in Spain. It could be a big selling point to tourists if marketed properly. Naturally it would have to be beneficial to you."

After a moment of quiet she heard his slow intake of breath, as if he carried a heavy weight few people would ever detect. It came from that dark place in his psyche. Though she didn't know the reason for it, she wanted to cry for his pain laid buried so deeply.

He slowly removed his arm and sat back in the seat. "Come home with me and we'll talk about it."

She turned to look at him again. "You mean *now*?"

"Sí, but I would understand if you're not feeling up to the drive yet."

"I've never felt better," she defended.

"*Bueno*. Until you've seen the estate from the inside, no meaningful discussion can take place. Since I need to get back, I suggest we take advantage of the time. As you just told me, you were going to spend the day working anyway."

"But that would mean you'd have to drive me back here later. It would be too much to ask."

"Believe me, anyone on my staff would be happy for a reason to escape."

His comment caused the corner of her mouth to turn up. "Are you such a dreadful boss?"

The devil was in the smile he flashed at her. "I'll let you be the judge. I should probably tell you ahead of time Diego would refuse his next paycheck for the privilege of escorting you anywhere."

Jillian felt her cheeks grow hot. "He was very obliging."

"I should imagine he and most men are, available or not."

Remi was warning her about something. "Is Diego married?"

"Sí. Dangerously so."

She laughed. "Dangerously?"

"With four children, his wife keeps very close tabs on him."

"He's very handsome, but she has no reason to fear a one-eyed American doing business with Count Goyo." She loved the way that sounded.

Out of the corner of her eye she saw his hands tighten on the steering wheel. "Before 1850 that title might have meant something, but no longer. I prefer you to think of me as Remi."

That was the fourth time he'd told her.

"Beware of something else, Senora. Your patch adds an intriguing element some might find irresistible."

"You've just given me an idea. If I find out I'm blind, I may have a set of designer patches made up in different colors to match my outfits. What do you think?"

"I think you're thinking too much," sounded his gravelly voice.

"I'm only planning ahead. You have to admit the tourists on my bus wouldn't have any trouble finding me in a crowd."

"Did they ever?"

"It's been known to happen."

She felt his gaze on her. "What do you do in that case?"

"I find *them*."

"In certain quarters that could also prove dangerous."

"My husband taught me some moves."

A strange sound came from his throat. "Now you've made me curious. When you are feeling stronger and the doctors say you can lower your head below your heart, you'll have to use me for a demonstration."

She turned to look out the passenger window. "I didn't say they worked on everyone."

"Shall we agree to reserve judgment until then?" he queried silkily.

They'd left the city and were traveling on the open road toward Toledo. She felt so alive it was painful. Somehow she needed to get hold of herself. When Remi had been wiping her tears a little while ago out of comfort, she'd come close to burying her face in his neck. She'd *wanted* to touch him.

The next time one of her friends tried to line her up, Jillian had better accept. Otherwise she was going to deserve the labels put on widows who couldn't control themselves when the first temptation came their way.

Except that he wasn't offering to satisfy her physical needs, not in that way. Since talking only seemed to get her into more trouble, she rested her head against the corner of the window and closed her eyes.

If Remi didn't keep his eyes straight ahead, there was going to be another accident in the same place on the highway. She insisted she'd never felt better, yet she'd been asleep for well over an hour. Jillian Gray needed many things, but above all she required rest. He would make certain she got it.

Her bravado only increased his fear that even a partial recovery from that freakish eye injury might not happen. When he'd heard her laughter in the face of such a possible loss, it ripped him apart. The idea of a patch covering up one of those beautiful eyes produced a groan from him. Unfortunately it was loud enough that Jillian's eyelid fluttered open. She looked the slightest bit disoriented.

"Welcome back, *Senora*."

Recovering quickly, she straightened in the seat. "H-how long have I been asleep?"

"We're almost to the entrance of the estate."

"I can't believe it."

"After what you've been through, *I* can." After a few more kilometers, he swung the car beneath the Gothic-type arched gate she'd passed two days ago.

Jillian undid her seat belt as they drove into a large, deep courtyard flanked by two residences reminiscent of the Ottoman Empire. The larger one beyond the fountain was a small palace. She gasped at the unmatchable plasterwork of the Mudejar style. Never had she seen more exquisite brick ornamentation.

"How absolutely beautiful…"

In her mind's eye she could picture those elegant Spanish carriages from the past pulled by dark spotted Appaloosa horses circling the ornate fountain in the center. To think Remi had been born here…all the fabulous tile work…the detail…roses everywhere…

She turned her head toward him. "When was your home built?"

"1610, to be exact."

Jillian shook her head in disbelief. "I bet this enthralls you every time you drive in."

Her enthusiasm was like an unexpected breath of fresh air.

"I can feel the heart of old Spain throbbing in my veins whispering her secrets." She sat back again, taking everything in. "If I lived here, I'd never want to leave."

"I try to stay here as much as possible."

In a small voice she said, "I take it something of vital importance brought you out of seclusion the other day."

"Correct, Senora."

It had been a day like none other. One moment Remi was driving along trying to absorb the first good news in two years, in the next he was plunged into a life and death situation with this remarkable woman whose inner strength continued to humble him.

He drove them to the front of the main house where he parked the car. "Welcome to La Rosaleda, Jillian," he said, helping her from the car.

She turned to him. "What does Rosaleda mean exactly?"

"The rose garden. The house has been called that for almost four hundred years. The indoor rose garden serves as an oasis in this dry heat."

His housekeeper opened the double doors and stepped forward to greet them.

"Maria? Meet Senora Jillian Gray from New York City," he said in English. "Jillian? Maria runs this house. She and her husband Paco live upstairs."

"Welcome, Senora." They shook hands.

"*Gracias,* Maria. It's a great pleasure for me."

"I prepared your room. Follow me."

"Just a moment, Maria."

To Remi's surprise his guest hurried around to the back of

the car. Before he could warn her not to bend over, she'd retrieved her brother's bouquet. She walked toward the housekeeper and handed the carnations to her.

"Knowing the Senor and how good he has been to me since the accident, I have no doubts he's asked you to go to a lot of trouble for me. I want you to have these as my way of saying thank you. If my brother were here, he would thank you too."

At Jillian's explanation Remi couldn't have been any more surprised than Maria. Her mouth suddenly broadened into a wide smile at their visitor. "*Muchas gracias, Senora.*"

"Call me Jillian, *por favor.*"

"J-Jil-yan?"

"That's *good.*"

Both women laughed in the face of Jillian's lie before Maria disappeared with the flowers.

Remi's mouth curved upward. "Flowers for Maria from a guest? That's a first for her. She won't forget your generosity."

"I'm the one imposing."

"Let's get you out of this heat, shall we? You'll find the thick walls keep house much cooler."

She accompanied him inside, but only took a few more steps before she let out another gasp and came to a halt.

Alarmed, he reached for her in case she was feeling light headed. "What's wrong? Are you ill?"

"No." She turned toward him. "Forgive me for startling you," she said, slowly easing her arm from his grasp. Every time he touched her now, he started a small fire.

"It's just that I've known private homes with honeycomb vaulting such as this existed, but I've only seen the rare pictures of them in books. Outside of the Alhambra I've explored, I never thought I'd be privileged to experience a true Spanish treasure first hand. It's like coming upon a mystical kingdom where Othello and Don Quixote would be at home."

Her explanation helped his muscles to relax. The description of his birthplace was very moving. Indeed it paralleled his own thoughts formed from the cradle, but never expressed aloud.

"When you've freshened up, we'll eat lunch in the patio room."

"That sounds lovely. For the first time in several days I'm actually hungry."

She followed him down a passageway of glazed, multicolored tiles to the right of the arched foyer. They had to be four hundred years old yet still retained their brilliant colors of blue, red, orange and green. Fabulous!

He came to a set of carved double doors with brass studs and opened them, revealing a magnificent room befitting a nobleman's house.

"The bathroom is through that door on the left. Make yourself at home. I'll be back with your suitcase. In case you've forgotten, it's time for your eyedrops."

He left her standing there bemused by her surroundings. In the midst of this kind of splendor, she *had* forgotten. A huge chandelier with real candles hung from the stalactite ceiling. At her feet lay an intricately inlaid wood floor in a striped Moorish design, making it difficult to know where to look first.

The big canopied bed of white lace would have dominated a smaller room. Her fascinated gaze passed from the brass wall sconces to the massive armoires and writing desk. The dark wood had been inlaid with mother-of-pearl, a long lost art.

In one end of the room she spied a round table of an unusual shade of yellow wood tinted with darker veining. Several ornately upholstered chairs in jewel tones surrounded it. At the other end she saw a grouping of damask love seats and an ottoman arranged around a fireplace.

Above the elaborately carved mantel hung an immense oil painting of a mature olive tree in full flower, its trunk gnarled and twisted. There was a plaque at the bottom. She moved closer to read it.

Gat Shemanim. The words were in Hebrew. What did they mean?

Her gaze flicked to the olive groves she could see from the window, then shifted back to the painting again. She could almost hear its silvery leaves rustling in the breeze, never realizing how fascinating an olive tree could be.

Senor Goyo had been tending them from boyhood, extracting the rich oil from their fruit revered by men over the centuries. The thought of him engaged in something so important throughout his whole life had a strange effect on her, moving her to tears for a reason she couldn't comprehend.

To her dismay he'd come back in the room with her suitcase and his flowers, catching her in another emotional moment.

She heard him pause before he lowered her bag to the floor and walked over to her. "What am I going to do with you?" he asked in a husky tone.

Jillian knew what she wanted him to do, but that would be the worst thing she could do for herself, and it would only embarrass him.

"Great beauty always makes me emotional." She tried to resist looking at him. "Tell me the meaning on the plaque of the painting."

He studied her face briefly before he said, "The Garden of Gethsemane. Several olive trees still growing there would have witnessed the Lord's suffering. My grandmother, devout in the faith, had it painted as a first anniversary gift for my grandfather. He insisted it hang in their bedroom. My parents kept up the tradition."

"So this was their room, too."

His dark head nodded. "Five generations of Goyos have slept in here."

She stared at him. "Does that mean you, too?"

Lines broke out on his hard-boned features alerting her she'd stepped onto sacred ground. That was the trouble with asking questions that were none of her business. In her need to learn more about him, all she managed to do was upset him.

"I live in the house to the north of the courtyard."

Not in the main house?

What terrible history had gone here to bring an end to traditions he clearly loved?

"Do you need a few more minutes alone?" he asked in a deceptively mild voice, but she wasn't fooled.

"Give me five minutes to put in my drops and I'll join you in the patio room. Where is it?"

"When you leave the bedroom, go left and you'll soon come to it." He put the flowers down on the bedside table and started to leave.

"Remi…" His black eyes swerved to hers. "Do you mind if I put the roses on that yellow table?"

"Why would I mind?" Before she could blink he'd done it for her.

"Thank you. It's such an exquisite piece of furniture and the flowers look gorgeous against it. What kind of wood is it?"

His eyes scrutinized her. "Can't you guess?"

"You mean that's from an olive tree?"

"Sí, Senora."

"I had no idea."

"When I was little my grandmother told me God loved the

olive tree best of all the trees He created. To hide its beauty from the other trees so they wouldn't be jealous, He gave it a flaw in the form of a gnarled trunk.

"She was a wise woman always trying to teach me, but I'm afraid I didn't appreciate the greatness of her wisdom until very recently."

Once Jillian was alone she pulled the drops from her purse to treat her eye. Throughout the process his haunting words refused to leave her alone. That was the way with riddles.

Like every riddle, it wanted solving…

CHAPTER FOUR

JILLIAN LEFT THE BEDROOM a few minutes later and followed the passageway to the end. It opened up into an exquisite garden. Palm trees surrounded a rectangular pool of azure blue, decorated with colorful tiles. A latticed roof of Ottoman design sheltered it from the full brunt of the sun.

She felt like she'd come upon an oasis in the middle of the desert, yet it was deep inside this great *casa*. Charmed beyond words, she moved closer toward the inviting water.

Once again her lungs constricted, but this time it was because she suddenly noticed Remi's sleek, powerful body maneuvering like a torpedo close to the floor of the pool. She watched in fascination while he did several laps before surfacing. He shook his head, sprinkling her unintentionally before he levered himself to the patio.

Jillian looked away, but it wasn't fast enough for him to catch her staring. His black trunks rode low on his hips, revealing most of his well-cut physique to her vision.

He reached for a towel hanging over the back of one of the chairs to dry off. The whiteness of the material looked exaggerated against the dark gold of his olive skinned body. His house might be a great work of art, but *so was he*.

"I would have invited you to join me, but Dr. Filartigua says no swimming, at least until he sees you again." He tossed the towel aside and shrugged into a short-sleeved cotton shirt he left unbuttoned. "Come and sit down." He pulled a chair away from the square-tiled table to help her.

"Thank you."

No sooner did he pull another chair around for himself than a dark-haired woman probably Jillian's age approached carrying a tray of food and drinks. Her curious brown eyes looked at both of them before she set it down on the table.

"*Gracias*, Soraya. Please meet my guest, Senora Jillian Gray."

She lifted her head. "How do you do, Senora."

"Soraya and her husband and children live in the house to the south of the courtyard."

"I'm pleased to meet you, Soraya."

Remi lifted everything off the tray before handing it back to her. His gaze swerved to Jillian. "Soraya is Paco and Maria's married daughter. She has two children, eight and six. Before the day is out you'll meet them and her husband, Miguel."

Jillian smiled at her. "I have a niece and nephew whom I miss terribly. What are your children's names?"

"Marcia and Nina."

"Perhaps you should warn them my eye got poked by some glass so they won't be scared when they first meet me and think I'm some kind of alien from outer space."

At Soraya's puzzled expression Remi translated for her. A smile broke out on her pretty face. She said something back in rapid Spanish. He turned to Jillian. "She says her girls will think you look like Cinderella."

"You mean from the fractured fairy tale version," she fairly mumbled so the other woman wouldn't pick up her words. She had to jest or go a little mad waiting for the result of her checkup next week.

Any light from Remi's gaze faded before he declared, "Senora Gray says you're too kind, Soraya."

Jillian's bad manners had not amused him. Horrified by her gaffe, she looked up at the other woman and nodded. What else could she do?

As soon as Maria's daughter left them alone, Remi began eating as if nothing had happened.

"I'm sorry," she whispered.

"I've been wondering when you would vent. It had to happen sometime. You wouldn't be human otherwise. We can only carry pain inside us for so long."

Her hand twisted the corner of the cloth napkin into a wad. "But not at Soraya's expense."

"She doesn't know enough English to have understood. No harm done."

"But *you* won't forget. After everything you've done for me, I'm ashamed."

He drank from his water goblet, then leveled his glance on her. "Don't be. I assume you would have made the same remark to your brother in front of her. Since I promised to stand in for him, it must mean I'm doing an adequate job."

Ping. Did you hear what he just said, Jillian?

"The next time I talk to Dave, I'll tell him that being taken care of by Senor Goyo is like having another protective brother around. I couldn't possibly be in better hands."

If she truly looked on him the way she did Dave, she wouldn't have given it a thought, but that wasn't the case. To be this aware of Remi was pure torture and she still had the rest of the day to get through before someone drove her back to Madrid.

She thought, of course, her comment would have pleased him, but those shuttered eyes revealed nothing to her gaze. He continued to eat without saying anything. Maybe she'd better concentrate on the food before he thought she wasn't hungry after all.

Trying not to look at him sitting there with a portion of his tanned chest showing, she took her first bites of food. "Um… is this lamb?"

"Sí, Senora. It's called *cuchifrito*."

"And what's the other dish?"

"*Queso manchego*, a local cheese specialty made from ewe's milk."

"Everything's delicious."

"I'm glad you approve."

Though he seemed to have a healthy appetite, there was an awkward silence between them she didn't know how to breach. It was her fault. Not knowing what else to do, she ate everything on her plate before putting down her fork.

"Remi?" she said at last. Her nerves were too frayed to sit there much longer like this. "Have you given any thought to my proposal?" He hadn't broached the subject yet, but maybe talking about business would get them on a better footing.

"Before a discussion can take place, you need to tour the estate. If you're up to it, we'll get started. I need to change and will meet you in the courtyard in fifteen minutes."

He put his napkin down and rose to his feet. She had the impression he couldn't get away from her fast enough. "Stay here and enjoy the dessert that's coming. Normally we would serve you oranges, a tradition of the Goyas. However, I asked Maria to prepare something unique for you."

She flashed him a small smile, hoping to ease the tension. "Another specialty of the region?"

"That's right. When you've finished, tell me if you don't prefer chocolate mousse made with olive oil rather than butter." On that parting note he disappeared through an alcove.

It turned out Jillian was late joining him.

The mousse was out of this world. She ended up following Soraya into the kitchen to have a discussion with Maria about how she'd made it. Jillian learned they used olive oil for everything.

"In Spain we're surrounded with olive groves, not dairy land." Her explanation made perfect sense.

"Did you put a little almond in the mousse?"

"No. Our olives have a fruity taste."

Fabulous. Jillian had cooked with Goyo oil many times, but hadn't realized how that particular flavor would come out in the chocolate. "I'd love to stay in here and talk, but the Senor is waiting. Thank you for the wonderful meal."

"Thank you for the flowers." She'd put them on a side table beneath the arched window.

After nodding to both women she hurried through the casa to get her digital camera. Then she ran out to the courtyard. Remi and one of his staff stood against the door of a truck with their heads together. He broke off talking when he saw her and moved toward her wearing jeans and a white cotton shirt his build did amazing things for.

"I'm sorry I'm late, but there was a reason," she explained nervously.

His worried gaze swept over her. "If you're too tired or hot, we can put this off."

"If you must know, I was in the kitchen talking to Maria and the time got away from us."

At her explanation, the frown lines around his eyes cleared up. "This is her husband, Paco." He made the introductions.

Jillian shook the foreman's hand. He had a full head of glistening black hair and was attractive like Diego. The Spanish were beautiful people.

"Your wife is a terrific cook."

"I know," he said in a teasing voice, patting his slight paunch. He made a playful fist against the boss's shoulder. "On this one it doesn't show."

No. The Senor was a breed apart from everyone else.

"See you later, Remi." He made a slight bow to her and walked toward the main house.

"If you'll get in the truck, I'll take you around the property so you can see if this is what you'd visualized. We won't do anything on foot because it's too hot."

"Would you still say that if I hadn't just had an operation?"

"No."

Well, that answer was direct enough.

"I have no desire to be forced to send for another helicopter because this time I allowed you to suffer heat exhaustion."

Her flushed cheeks darkened in color. "You weren't responsible for what happened to me."

"I'm responsible now," came the obdurate response, bringing out the dark side in his nature. "Shall we go?"

He opened the door and helped her inside. She wasn't able to prevent the hem of her dress riding up her thigh. The attempt to pull it down came too late. His dark eyes didn't miss anything before she moved her sandaled foot inside so he could shut the door.

Remi climbed in the other side. When he started the motor, the air conditioner came on, much to her relief. He drove them behind the main house to the area where she could see a large number of outbuildings. The complex was more like a living museum and much bigger than she'd imagined.

"This is a part of the estate we don't use anymore. You're looking at the spot where Soleado Goyo had its earliest beginnings."

"What does Soleado mean exactly?"

"Sunny, like your hair."

The personal comment confused her. Sometimes at his most distant, he inserted some remark that quickened her pulse. Jillian forced herself to concentrate as he pointed out the old mill house and the primitive olive press house with its orange-tiled roof and tower. With the huge shade trees, she found the whole scene had an old world charm all its own, like a painting. She drew out her camera and began snapping pictures.

A little farther on beneath the trees they came upon a well and, beyond it, a barn. He drove the truck to the opening, where she could see one of those gorgeous black carriages from the past she'd envisioned being drawn around the courtyard. Near the entrance she noticed half a dozen huge antique storage jars once used to hold the precious oil.

"The moving and lifting in those days must have been backbreaking work," she cried.

"It still is," he muttered. "The only difference is that the oil processing and packaging is done in air-conditioned buildings. It might interest you to know that many of the homes in the region didn't have ovens because of the heat. Fried foods ruled the day, making olive oil a necessity."

She couldn't learn enough. Everything he told her would be fascinating to tour groups.

They drove through several miles of neat rows of olive trees, providing her an unforgettable sight. "The harvest won't take place until December," he said, reading her mind.

"Do you use machines for that?"

"We grow the *cornicabra* olives. They must be handpicked in order to make extra virgin oil."

"Cornicabra?"

His lips curved. Once again he seemed amused by her inquisitive nature. "The olives are pointed like a goat's horn."

"There's so much to learn. It would take a lifetime."

"*Sí*, Senora," he answered.

He sounded so far away just then, it struck her that this personal guided tour was the last thing he'd wanted to do with his busy day. Because of his misplaced sense of guilt over the car accident, he'd taken several days off from his work to see to her welfare and now *he* was playing tour guide.

While she sat there deep in thought, he drove on until they came to the newer buildings now in use to receive the olives and make the oil. Another one did the bottling, still another prepared the crates for shipping within the country and abroad. He had a huge concern to run.

It dawned on her that if there'd been no accident, she had a gut feeling she wouldn't have gotten to even speak with him over the phone. Once she'd introduced herself as representing EuropaUltimate Tours and had explained her reason for wanting to talk to him, no doubt he would have been congenial, but he wouldn't have had the time or the inclination to entertain the idea of tour buses stopping at his property.

This wasn't a winery where the tourists could get off the bus and enter a wine cellar for a tasting party. Any visit guaranteed that the tourists would need a bathroom, a cold drink and respite from the heat. Without those amenities, she couldn't possibly make this stop part of a day's activity for the people in her charge.

Remi already knew that. It was the reason why he'd told her they couldn't discuss business until after she'd seen the estate. He wasn't set up to accommodate tour groups, but instead of giving her a flat-out no, he'd allowed her to figure it out for herself.

Her host always managed to do everything right, but she felt the fool. If her company hadn't included an olive grove on their tour itineraries long before now, she should have known there was a practical reason why. Leave it to her to get so caught up in the excitement, she couldn't see beyond the end of her nose.

Maybe her accident had impaired her thinking along with her vision. Intruding on his time had already inconvenienced the Senor, though he'd never admit it.

She shifted in her seat, glad the truck tour was over. Besides everything else, being confined in the cab with Remi made her cognizant of everything masculine about him. Jillian needed to be gone from Soleado Goyo as soon as possible. Hopefully he'd meant it when he'd said one of his staff would be glad to drive her back to Madrid. She couldn't take being alone with this incredible man any longer.

She felt his dark gaze slant her way. "Had enough?"

That was no idle question. He couldn't wait for this experience to be over with so he could get on with his normal life. Jillian lowered her head, wondering what he'd do if she told him she could never have enough of him. Instead she said, "I've enjoyed every minute of it, but I confess I'm ready to go back."

"I thought so."

She thought she heard relief in his tone before he circled around and headed home, nodding to several workers walking to their cars. Not much longer now and he'd be a free man. He was probably counting the minutes until he didn't have to feel responsible for her. If he hadn't talked to David, none of this would be happening.

As she sat there staring blindly out the passenger window, she could feel a strange tension building between them. To save him the necessity of having to spell things out for her, she decided to jump in and get it over with.

"I want to thank you for showing me around the estate. It's an experience I wouldn't have missed. The next time I'm back in my apartment in New York and have friends over for dinner, I'll tell them about this incredible day while they enjoy chocolate mousse made from your *cornicabra* olive oil. Maria gave me the recipe. They won't believe how good it is."

"That won't be happening for a while," came his dampening response.

"True," she said in a quiet tone. The doctor had warned her no flying for a whole month, but that didn't mean she couldn't take a train to the charming town of Cáceres and stay there until the week was out. Anything to get away from the temptation... Tomorrow she would be on the first train that headed in that direction.

By the time they'd reached the courtyard, the sun had dropped much lower in the sky. They'd been gone longer than she'd realized.

He pulled up in front of the main house where she could see whom she believed to be Soraya's children playing on scooters. Remi didn't appear to notice. With the engine still idling for the benefit of the air conditioning, he turned to her.

"You need to rest. In a little while we'll have a light supper and then talk business."

She clasped her hands. "Remi, you've bent over backwards for me the last few days. I can't thank you enough for everything, including this tour of the estate, but after seeing it for myself I realize what I was asking for is impossible."

"Say that again?" His words sounded like ripping silk, alerting her something was wrong.

"Soleado Goyo isn't a hotel. I don't know what I was thinking when I suggested a tour bus could stop here. You don't have the facilities for tourists wandering around needing bathrooms and drinks." She shook her head. "It simply wouldn't work, but being the person you are you were unselfish enough to give up your personal time to show me around so I could draw my own conclusions.

"I'm very grateful, Remi, but now it's time for me to leave. If you'll let whoever's driving me to Madrid know I'm ready, I'll just run inside to freshen up first."

Without waiting for his response, Jillian climbed out of the truck, needing to put as much distance between them as possible.

"Hola!" she said to the children who answered in kind, eyeing her curiously before she rushed past them to enter the house. She heard footsteps behind her and thought they'd followed her, but when she turned around she discovered it was Remi who'd come into the master bedroom.

He shut the door and leaned against it, staring at her with a disturbing glint in his eyes. "Where's the fire, Jillian?"

She swallowed hard, unable to sustain that look. "I don't know what you mean."

When she saw him fold his strong arms, a shiver ran through her body.

"What's the reason you suddenly have to get back to Madrid? You haven't had anything to eat or drink yet."

"I'm still full from lunch, and since my business with you is concluded, it's only fair to the person driving me to get an early start so they can be back at a decent hour."

At this point he'd moved away from the door. Standing there with his hard-muscled legs slightly apart, he reminded her how impossibly attractive he was, reinforcing the reason why she shouldn't stay here another second.

"What makes you think we don't have business to talk over?"

She rubbed her palms against womanly hips, a gesture he

observed with those intense black eyes. "I—I don't understand." What was he getting at?

His chest rose and fell visibly. "I'll be back in a few minutes to explain."

Knowing he always meant what he said, the second he went out the door she hurried into the bathroom. No sooner did she emerge than there was a knock on her door.

She trembled before opening it. Soraya stood at the entry with a tray.

"The Senor told me to put this on the table."

Jillian smiled at her. "Come in."

She moved quickly and set it down. Her eyes darted from the roses to Jillian. "You have beautiful flowers."

"I agree." It was on the tip of her tongue to tell her Remi had brought them to the hospital. However, at the last second she held back from divulging that revelation in case Soraya misunderstood the reason. "Thank you."

The other woman nodded. No doubt she'd drawn her own conclusions.

On her way out of the room she passed Remi. Once the door was closed, he walked over to the table. "Come and join me," he said, flicking her a glance.

This wasn't a good idea. He had no conception of what his nearness was doing to her, but she couldn't very well refuse him. After helping her to sit down, he took his place opposite her.

Maria had prepared a light meal of salad with chicken. Most people in Spain didn't eat dinner before nine, but she realized Remi had made an exception for her. He was incredibly thoughtful, even providing ice water. She drank thirstily. Remi observed every move.

Halfway through their meal he put down his fork and sat back. "It's true the estate was never meant to be anything but my family's home and workplace. In order for me to accommodate the needs of the kind of tour you're talking about, new facilities would be required."

She wiped the corner of her mouth with the napkin. "I realize that. When I saw the groves, I'm afraid I got too carried away with excitement to consider the fundamental things required to make my plan feasible. To be honest, I'm embarrassed."

After a slight pause, "Would it surprise you to know you're the first person to broach such an idea with me?" he queried. "It would never have entered my mind otherwise."

She squirmed in the chair. "All the more reason you should have pointed out the flaw in my plan and saved yourself the trouble of driving me all the way here. This is the third day you've had to worry about me instead of doing your work."

"Let's just say I was struck by your interest and your enthusiasm for something that's a living part of me. You have no call to be embarrassed, Jillian. In fact, you've given me an idea."

Her eyes widened in surprise. "What do you mean?"

He rubbed the side of his hard jaw with his hand. "I haven't told you why I went to Toledo the other day."

"No, but you indicated it was important."

"That's true. This has been one of the driest years on record. There isn't going to be enough rain in the coming months to fill the reservoirs."

She nodded. "Someone in the office told us Spain hasn't had normal rainfall in a long time."

"Forty percent less," he informed her. "In Castile-La Mancha some of the reserves are as low as thirteen percent, and the government has imposed water restrictions. In some places the country has depended on tankers for their water."

Jillian shook her head. "How awful."

"We need heavy rain, but it probably won't happen." He pushed himself away from the table and walked over to the window, where she could see the groves in the distance. As he looked out at the vista he said, "In the last eight months there've been massive crop failures."

"On your estate, too?"

Lines marred his hard features. "We've had our share along with fires."

"Were they devastating?" she asked, her voice throbbing.

He turned to her. "They could have been. Fortunately on our property we have emergency wells we've opened as a last resort. However, as my accountant pointed out the other day, I'd be wise to diversify as an insurance policy against more hard times to come. At the time I'm afraid I didn't give him much heed in that department."

She rose to her feet, clinging to the chair. "Why?"

A nerve throbbed along his jawline. "My parents grew other crops that could be harvested at a different time of the year to bring in income, but they too were afflicted with droughts and it became a doomed project."

She could hear what he wasn't saying, that he and his family had worked unceasingly without the expected results. Her heart went out to him.

"For the last two years I've been working with a skeleton crew to reverse our losses."

"And have you recovered?" She held her breath waiting for his answer.

His gaze collided with hers before he nodded. "I've finally rounded the corner."

"So the other day you were driving home from Toledo filled with the joy of that knowledge, only to be run off the road by a crazy American driver whose mind was on your olive groves. An idiot who didn't have the sense she was born with to avoid catastrophe!"

Her little sob resounded in the air. In the next instant Remi closed the distance between them. She felt arms of velvet steel go around her.

Without saying anything he rocked her back and forth the way her husband would have done if he'd been there. The contact caused the floodgates to open. She sobbed against his broad shoulder and clung to him, unaware of the passage of time.

Jillian was crying over so many things she didn't know where one pain left off and another began. It was all mixed together with Remi's own pain. He whispered words she didn't understand, but they comforted her. Somehow—she didn't know quite how—she ended up lying full length on the bed without remembering being carried there. Slowly the tears subsided and she felt his weight as he sat down next to her. His fingers smoothed the tear-moistened hair off her brow and temples.

"Lie still." His voice was soft. "I'll change the dressing on your eye."

It was like déjà vu. She lay on the ground at the side of the road and he was kneeling over her, urging her to be calm until help arrived.

With aching tenderness he eased the wet strips of tape off her face and pulled the patch away.

She looked up into those black pools tinged with concern and something else she couldn't decipher. "I can't see anything out of my right eye. Is it still there?"

That pulse at his jaw was throbbing again. "I'll prove it," he said deep in his throat. Then he lowered his head and kissed both her eyes like a benediction. The gesture reassured her as nothing else could have done.

"Forgive me for falling apart on you," she said, her voice trembling.

Their breath mingled. "I'm glad you did. Now I know you're not superhuman. For a while I wondered."

Her eyes filled with liquid once more. "Thank you, Remi."

"If you start crying again, the new tape I'm trying to put on you will get soaked," he said, gently teasing her.

She bit her bottom lip. "I'll be good."

Remi blotted her eyelids with a tissue, then proceeded to affix the patch. "How does that feel?"

"You do excellent work, Doctor."

A smile like none other broke the corner of his sensuous mouth. And for the first time, there was no darkness in it. When he looked like that, she could feel herself falling through space.

"You have magic in your touch. I bet your olive trees love you."

To her chagrin his expression sobered.

"Did I say something wrong?"

"No," he murmured. "You just reminded me of something my father used to say when I was a boy."

"What was that?" She wanted to know all there was to know about him.

"The trees are alive, Remigio. Be gentle with them."

"I believe that."

There was an electric current flowing between them, but all too soon he got up from the bed. The last thing she wanted was for him to walk away.

He checked his watch before staring down at her. "Right now I have a meeting with Diego that can't be put off. Stay the night, Jillian. Tomorrow we'll talk about an idea I have in mind that could be good for EuropaUltimate Tours and solve a problem for me at the time same."

Joy arced through her body. Another night with him, this time under *his* roof…She knew she shouldn't, but she was dying to know what was going on inside his head. In the end her curiosity won out over common sense. Since meeting him, she didn't have any.

"If I'm going to stay, I'd better call the Prado Inn and cancel my reservation."

Her capitulation seemed to please him. "The phone's right there at your bedside. See you in the morning. *Buenas noches.*"

Once he'd left she phoned the Prado, then called her brother's cell. He answered on the second ring.

"Hi, Dave. It's moi."

"It's about time. I just called your hotel and they told me you hadn't checked in yet. You should be in bed. What's going on?"

"Actually I *am* in bed, just not in Madrid."

"Where then?"

"I'm being waited on hand and foot at the Soleado Goyo. The Senor put me in the master bedroom."

There was a long silence. "Jilly…honey…do you know what you're doing?" he asked quietly. "Is he married?"

"I don't think so."

"You mean, you don't know?"

"No, I don't, and he hasn't offered any information."

"I don't like it."

She grinned. "First you tell me I need to start living again and now you think I'm living a life of debauchery. You can't have it both ways, brother dear."

"Come on, Jilly—"

"Dave, calm down. I'm in his parents' old bedroom. He doesn't even sleep in the main house."

"What do you mean 'main' house?"

"Remi's full name is Count Remigio Goyo."

"Count— As in—"

"The Spanish aristrocracy. The Goyo estate is huge and so fabulous you can't believe it. He has his own house besides the main one, and there's a third house. I don't know who lives there."

He muttered something unintelligible, but she could read his mind.

"I'll pretend I didn't hear that."

"Just remember he has the master key to the place. The 'droit de Seigneur' thing will always be alive."

"Not in the 21st century! And don't you know I'm a one-eye monstrosity wearing a patch? That's how I know I'm safe." That plus the fact that he was always the gentleman.

"How long are you going to stay there?" He still sounded unconvinced.

"We're going to talk business in the morning, then someone will drive me back to Madrid."

"How far away is it?"

She chuckled. "What is this? Twenty questions?"

"Look, Jilly, you just had an operation and can't come home yet. Naturally I'm concerned."

"I know," she said, "and I love you for caring, but honestly I'm fine. If you want to know the truth, he makes me feel cherished."

"Jilly? How are you? Honestly?"

"I'm much better than I expected to be." Breaking down in his arms seemed to have accomplished something nothing else could. Three times now he'd kept her from going off the deep end.

"Okay then. Look after yourself. 'Night."

"Love you and send my kisses to the children and Angela."

After hanging up Jillian quickly prepared for bed. Being a

tour guide had helped her learn to sleep anywhere with little trouble. However, sleeping in this room was a privilege. Her mind wouldn't turn off.

After her conversation with her brother, she decided that first thing tomorrow she would ask Remi a few questions and not just for her brother's sake. It wasn't fair the Senor knew almost every intimate thing about her. She felt she could tell Remi her deepest secrets, her darkest fears—but she knew nothing about his personal life.

The next morning while Jillian was finishing the breakfast Soraya had brought in earlier, she heard a knock on the door. Just thinking it might be Remi turned her insides to jelly.

"Come in."

Maria popped her head inside the door. "*Buenos dias,* Jillian."

"*Buenos dias*, Maria."

"The Senor wants you to come to the living room. I'll show you where it is. A police lieutenant is here about the car accident."

"That's right. I'd forgotten all about it." After finishing the last bite of roll, she followed Maria down the hall to the foyer and opened the double doors.

Two men stood talking in the center of a room even more fantastic than the master bedroom. One man was in uniform, but Jillian never noticed him. She was too busy feasting her gaze on the devastatingly attractive male wearing thigh-molding jeans and a creamy shirt. He'd dominated her dreams all night.

CHAPTER FIVE

REMI'S PULSE RACED WHEN he saw a golden-haired figure enter the room. Some American women carried themselves with a certain confidence that made them stand out. She would have anyway, he mused to himself.

The short-sleeved khaki blouse gave definition to the slenderly rounded body he'd held close to him last night. Her imprint had left an indelible impression, causing him a restless night.

Up to now he'd only seen her in a dress or a skirt and blouse. This morning she'd put on matching khaki pants that outlined her long, shapely legs. Judging by the way the officer couldn't take his eyes off her, he, too, was mesmerized by her femininity. There ought to be a law…

"Senora Gray?"

As she looked at him, her eye glowed green fire in a room of dark, heavy furniture. Gone were last night's tears. Their presence had revealed unexpected vulnerabilities that squeezed his heart.

"This is Captain Perez. He wants to ask you a few questions about the accident."

She turned her attention to the other man. "How do you, Captain." They shook hands.

"It won't take long, Senora. If you'd prefer to sit—"

"I'm fine."

Remi watched him study her the way any man would when confronted by exceptional beauty. For a reason he didn't wish to examine, it bothered him much more than it should have.

"I'm sorry your eye was injured, but I must confess I'm relieved to see you are looking so well."

"Thank you. Senor Goyo is responsible for my quick recovery. My own family couldn't have taken better care of me, had they been able to be here."

The furrow deepened between Remi's brows. Did Jillian know about her sister-in-law's precarious condition?

"You are most fortunate, Senora. For the record, what I need from you is an account of how the accident happened."

Remi listened as she told her version. It didn't vary from his own except that she took full blame for it by explaining her bad judgment in trying to swerve her car.

The officer nodded and wrote a few words in his notebook. Then he lifted his head. "I understand you work for EuropaUltimate Tours. Why is it that you were alone in a rental car that day?"

"Between bus tours I do research to plan new tours for the company."

"You were planning a tour here in Castile-La Mancha?"

"Yes."

He smiled. "In this time of drought, tourism is good for our country."

Jillian's gaze flicked to Remi before she said, "In my opinion this part of Spain is one of the true wonders of the world."

While Remi felt a rush of adrenaline infiltrate his system, the captain flashed a white smile. "I will pass your sentiment along, Senora. Thank you for your time."

"I'd like to thank you and all the people who came to my rescue so fast."

"Let us hope your eye heals completely."

She nodded, not allowing her smile to fade even though Dr. Filartigua had indicated that such a miracle wasn't going to happen.

"I'll see you out, Captain." Remi was anxious for the officer to leave before he said anything more damaging. Jillian didn't need to dwell on the negative, and he wanted to get to the bottom of a certain comment she'd made a few moments ago.

She joined him in the foyer to see the officer out the door. When he'd gone, Remi turned to her. "You look like you slept well."

"I did." Her gaze took in the foyer's accoutrements. "This is the lap of luxury for me. Breakfast brought in before I even asked for it. You've spoiled me."

If he hadn't been there when she'd broken down last evening, he could be forgiven for thinking she was invincible.

"But you still miss your brother," he inserted. Not to mention her deceased husband, whom he tried hard not to think about at all.

"Naturally I'd love to see him, but he couldn't come."

"Is that what he told you?"

"Dave didn't have to say anything. With Angela this close to her delivery date, he needs to be with her. If she weren't expecting, he would have flown over with her and the children." Her delicately arched brows formed a frown. "Why are you so concerned about that?"

Maybe she didn't know about the toxemia. Relieved by her explanation he said, "Probably because I haven't had a sister to worry about before." *Just keep thinking of her in those terms, Goyo.*

"She'd be a lucky woman," Jillian whispered.

While he digested that remark she asked, "What about brothers?"

He'd known this moment would come. "I have *one*," he muttered.

She looked away. "I'm sorry if my question was off-limits."

Remi inhaled sharply. "It was a perfectly normal question."

"But you'd prefer not to talk about him."

"Did I say that?" he challenged.

"You didn't have to."

He raked a hand through his hair. "What would you like to know?"

She hunched her feminine shoulders. "Only what you're willing to tell me."

His guest said and did everything right. "Let's take a walk outside before the heat becomes too intense. I have something important to discuss with you. Do you need to go back to your room first?"

"No. I'm ready."

A woman who didn't fuss. She was a rarity in too many disturbing ways.

He opened the door for her, unable to avoid breathing her fragrance as she moved past him to step outside. His eyes took in the exciting mold of her body before he caught up to her.

"Where are we going?" she asked without looking at him.

"If you're up for it, I'd like to go as far as the mill house I showed you yesterday."

"I'd love it. I'm a tour guide who's not used to such inactivity. It'll feel good to stretch my legs."

Remi immediately pushed the thought of her legs away.

They walked around the side of the main house. "His name is Javier."

"Older or younger?" she asked without missing her stride.

"Younger by thirteen months."

They kept on going. He paced his steps so she could keep up with him.

"I take it he's not on the estate. Where does he live?"

"That's a good question."

She slowed down and turned toward him with a stunned expression. "You really don't know?"

They'd reached the shade near the old olive press. He stared down at the woman looking so intently at him with her uncovered eye. He rubbed the back of his neck absently.

"Aside from two chance encounters, I haven't seen him since the day my wife ran off with him two years ago."

Jillian felt like someone had just run her through with a Toledo sword, the kind tourists paid a great deal of money to possess.

How did anyone recover from such a profound betrayal?

Much as she wanted to comfort him the way he'd comforted her over the last few days, she knew he would see it as a gesture of pity. Since she despised being the object of that horrid emotion, she kept her hands and arms to herself.

"You did ask," sounded a voice, so dark and hollow, it could have come from an underground cavern.

"That's me," she muttered in self-deprecation. "Fearless."

Without waiting for him she began walking again. He followed at a short distance until they reached the barn. She wished she were alone. Right now she was bleeding all over the place and there was nowhere to hide.

"I've had a year longer than you to deal with my emotions, Jillian."

That was meant to reassure her? If she'd had a sister who decided to run off with Kyle...

She swung around to face him, trying to imagine his anguish. "The difference is, up to the minute I lost my husband we were very happy, and I still have my brother w-while your bro—"

Jillian couldn't go on. She couldn't comprehend the magnitude of his pain. How did anyone handle that kind of hurt? Without conscious thought she moved inside the spacious barn where she attempted to recover her composure. He was pacing.

"Were you married a long time?"

He stopped. "Ten months."

Such a short time…What woman in her right mind would leave Remi? As far as Jillian was concerned, neither his brother or his wife were worthy to breathe the same air he did.

"Were you and Javier in business together?" she asked before she could stop herself.

"Si, Senora."

In that case it wasn't the drought problem alone. Remi had been forced to recoup his father's losses without Javier's help while at the same time dealing with the bitterness and heartache of losing the woman he'd married. She'd gone away with his own flesh and blood— It was too awful.

Jillian sucked in her breath, wishing she hadn't asked him if he had brothers. The answer had torn her apart. To delve any deeper into his personal life could only bring him more grief. It was time to change the subject.

She hugged her arms to her waist. "Now that we're out here, what was it you wanted to talk to me about?"

In the semidarkness she could feel his eyes scrutinizing her. "Much as I dislike the idea of doing anything other than what I know, I need to safeguard the future of the estate with another source of income." After a pause, he said, "Needless to say it won't be crops." He was talking as if she weren't there.

Jillian had already gathered that. She lifted her head and waited.

"It's strange that on the same day my accountant again brought up the subject of my diversifying, you happened along with your request. I've been mulling it over in my mind ever since." His hands slid to his back hip pockets. "Tell me something. How many people are on your tour buses at a time?"

"Twenty-eight including the driver and two tour guides."

One dark brow quirked. "I thought they were double that size."

"Most of them are, but our company believes a luxury tour must begin with less people to give them more one-on-one attention. A group of twenty-four, twenty-five tourists is much more manageable."

He nodded, then looked around the interior. "This mill house, the barn and olive press house were built to last, but they've been standing vacant and unused for years. I've been thinking…"

So had she!

From the moment he'd given her the tour yesterday her mind had leaped with ideas that had prevented her from falling asleep.

"They would be perfect," she whispered without realizing she'd spoken.

Remi folded his arms. Maybe it was a trick of light but she thought she saw his lips twitch. "I haven't said anything yet."

She chuckled. "Forgive me if I'm several leaps ahead of you."

"I'd like to hear what goes on in that mind of yours during one of those leaps."

She shook her head, embarrassed. "Please finish what you were about to say."

"*Muy bien*. I was going to ask a question. How many times during the summer would you anticipate one of your tour groups stopping here?"

"That would be entirely up to you. There's such a huge call for Spanish tourism all year round, I can conceive of as many tours as you could handle."

"Give me a number."

"Using Madrid or Toledo as the hub, I can envision hundreds within a year."

"That many?" He sounded surprised.

"It's easily possible if you did four a week. EuropaUltimate is one of the biggest on the continent. Tourists want everything from a grand tour of five weeks down to an overnight excursion. The lure of visiting the Soleado Goyo olive groves would be one of those unforgettable highlights."

"Your company has the perfect ambassador in you, Jillian."

"Thank you." She was inordinately pleased by the compliment. "Before we go any further, let me give you a ballpark figure of what you could make in a year with say a hundred and fifty stops. Depending on the scope of your financial goal, it should tell you if a venture like this would be worthwhile."

She told him and then held her breath waiting for a reaction. He was quiet so long she said, "Isn't it even close to what you'd need?"

He studied her features for a moment. "On the contrary. It would supplement things very nicely."

Her heartbeat sped up. "But—" She'd heard one in there somewhere. He had to have many reservations.

"I'm thinking of the winter months during the harvest."

"After what I learned from you yesterday, I factored that in. Naturally you can't be worried about tourists at such a critical time. The figure I quoted was based on nine months, leaving out December through February."

His intelligent eyes flashed her a glance that said he was

impressed. *And interested.* She was jumping out of her skin with excitement. He really was considering it.

"Will you show me inside the mill house?"

"Do you read minds, too?" His unexpected question provoked a smile from her, which he returned. She was thankful for that. Minutes ago his austerely handsome face had been a study in pain. "I was about to take you inside."

They moved in companionable silence toward the building with its attached storage shed. He opened the heavy wooden door. A heavy giant oak beam ran the length of the rectangular room. The millstones were still in place.

"Oh— This is fantastic!" Ideas were pouring into her head faster than she could contain them.

"If you're this taken with it, then you'll like our next stop. Come with me."

She followed him to the other house with its unique tower and charming mullioned windows. Once inside, she marveled over the ancient olive press. It was still intact. "You've kept everything in such beautiful condition," she exclaimed in a daze.

The wood flooring of these buildings and the barn had a patina built up over years of use. She touched the thick plastered walls with their beamed ceilings. They were the real thing. Combined with the influence of Moorish and Gothic architecture, her mind was flooded with flashes of *El Cid* and Philip of Spain.

She glanced over at him. "Any tourist privileged enough to step foot on your property will be swept back in history and never want to leave. Will you be able to handle that?"

He cocked his head. There was a mysterious look in his eyes. "Suppose we find out."

Jillian could hardly breathe.

"I'm an olive tree farmer, not a carpenter or a tour guide.

I know the exact moment to pick the olives for their oil, but I wouldn't know where to start with these relics. You know what you need and what will work, so here's my proposition... Why don't you stay here and sketch out some ideas for me? Use the writing desk in your bedroom and take all the time you need.

"While I'm at work, make La Rosaleda your home. Feel free to spend time wandering around the property to come up with your plans. When you need transportation, I'll arrange for it. On the drive to Madrid I'll be able to give you my full attention. We'll talk everything over then and I'll look at your ideas. Does that meet with your approval?"

Four more days to be with him legitimately...She would take them and hug them to herself. Part of her knew she should walk away, but already she found she couldn't.

Now that she knew his dark painful secret, she wanted to help him any way she could. It would take years for him to put a tragedy like he'd lived through behind him, but if she could bring even a modicum of peace to his mind through financial means, then she wanted to do it. She owed him.

"Thank you, Remi. I'll take you up on your gracious invitation since I'll need that long to do a thorough job." Aware he'd given her too much individual time already she said, "Please don't let me keep you from your work. I'm going to stay here for a while."

"If you're sure you'll be all right."

"I promise I won't overdo it."

His eyes narrowed. "I'm going to hold you to that. Maria will be serving lunch at noon. You can eat by the pool or in your room."

It didn't sound like he'd be joining her. What did she expect for heaven's sake? He was her boss now, not her rescuer.

"How about the kitchen? Maria and I have something in common because I enjoy cooking, too. I'd like to pick up some tricks from her. She's a pro."

A gorgeous smile broke from him, transforming his severe expression. It robbed her of breath. "I'll pass on your remarks. It will delight her, especially when she already has a high opinion of you. *Hasta despues,* Jillian."

He walked away. With every stride of his long, powerful legs her heart ached a little more for his suffering.

What kind of a woman would wound Remi that way? He was a man of such noble character and depth, she couldn't imagine his wife not loving him beyond reason.

Affairs happened, but not like this…

Intuition told her that Javier had never measured up to Remi. No man could. She could imagine that in his pathetic jealousy and selfishness of his elder brother, Javier had found a soul mate in Remi's shallow wife. Together they'd broken Godly covenants without counting the cost, but they hadn't broken the Senor.

Through power that came from his soul, he'd risen above their perfidy. With sheer grit and determination he'd been triumphant in protecting his heritage. Betrayed in the ugliest way possible, he hadn't let it destroy his life.

Any other man would have been lost in despair by now. She knew he carried the scars, but they hadn't destroyed him.

Not Remi.

Her admiration for him couldn't be measured. To think she came so close to hitting him with her car. A shudder passed through her body, not wanting to contemplate that tragedy.

After one more look around, she left the olive press house and walked outside with no particular destination in mind. Before she knew it, she found herself at the barn. The carriage beckoned her closer.

Had Remi ever ridden in it with his family?

Several years earlier one of the tour buses had stopped in Seville for the city's famous spring festival. Jillian still had photos of those lantern-lined streets. Hundreds of black carriages passed by filled with dark-haired senoritas in colorful flamenco dresses. The men were equally gorgeous in their black, form-fitting suits and hats set at jaunty angles.

Bemused by thoughts of Remi dressed to the hilt in such thrilling masculine attire with those black eyes flashing, she climbed into the open carriage and sat back in the leather seat, not ready to let go of her daydream quite yet.

What would it be like to ride in this with him on such an occasion? She rested her head against the back and closed her eyes, but when she imagined herself sitting proudly next to him, the fantasy stopped. A blond American with one eye was bad enough, but a blonde American with one eye dressed in a flamenco outfit would be simply beyond the pale. She sat forward again, making a sound of disgust in her throat.

That's when she heard giggling. She glanced at the open doorway and saw Soraya's two little girls standing together watching her.

Jillian chuckled. The crazy American woman made a ridiculous sight all right. With a smile, she motioned for them to join her. "Come and sit," she said in Spanish.

They rushed toward her needing no urging. After they'd taken the seat opposite her she leaned forward. "Which one of you is Marcia?"

The older girl looked surprise Jillian knew her name. She lifted her hand like she was in school. Jillian transferred her gaze to the younger one. "Then you must be Nina."

"*Sí.*"

They were adorable. "Shall we ask the Senor to take us for a ride?"

Their eyes rounded as if the question shocked them.

"Haven't you ever ridden in it?"

They shook their heads.

"Why not?"

Their little shoulders shrugged.

"Does the Senor have horses?"

"Sí." This from Marcia. "He keeps them at his work."

"Ah. Then I'll ask him tonight. Would you like that?"

The broad smiles they gave her provided the answer. Then Marcia spoke up again. "Mama told us to get you. Lunch is ready."

Already?

She checked her watch. She'd been out here a lot longer than she'd realized. If she wasn't mistaken, Remi had told the women to keep a close eye on her. Jillian had to admit it was nice to be watched over. In fact she could grow to like it too much. Normally it was her job to look after other people.

"Let's go."

They jumped down and she followed. At the doorway to the barn she reached for their hands. She did it without thinking because they reminded her of her own family. They seemed happy about it. Together they walked back to the main house. By the time they reached the foyer she had an idea.

"Would you like to eat your lunch with me in my room?"

They nodded excitedly and ran off to ask their mother. While they were gone she hurried to the bedroom and put in her eyedrops. Before long Soraya appeared with Jillian's tray. The girls trailed behind with their own.

"Do you mind if they eat with me?" she asked in Spanish.

"No, no. They're very excited."

"So am I. You have no idea how much I miss my own family."

"Of course."

"Would you like to eat with us, too?"

Soraya shook her head. "Not this time." She waved good-bye to her daughters and left the room. In another minute the three of them were gathered around the yellow table. The girls chattered a mile a minute. Jillian couldn't follow all their conversation but it didn't matter. Their presence was very comforting.

She found herself wondering who provided the balm to the Senor's troubled soul, but thinking about him got her into trouble. In a deliberate attempt to concentrate on something else, she got up from the table and went over to her suitcase.

Her clothes had been put away, but she'd left the gifts for the children inside it. Since she wasn't going to be seeing them for a while, she decided to give them to Marcia and Nina.

Removing the adaptor from her laptop, she plugged it into the little portable CD player she'd bought for them. She'd purchased several CDs in Spanish. One of them was a cartoon. Since Dave's children loved the English version so much and had it memorized, she knew they'd get a kick out of it.

The girls grew silent as she plugged it into the wall socket and placed it on the table. Once she turned it on, the girls became so engrossed in the charming story they forgot to eat. When their mother came to get them, they begged to stay long enough to finish it.

"I'll send them out when it's over," Jillian promised her. "In the meantime let me help take everything back to the kitchen." But Soraya insisted on doing it.

Too soon the movie was over. The girls didn't want to leave. However, they were too well-behaved to argue with their mother. Jillian sent the player and the other CDs with them, and invited them to eat lunch with her by the pool tomorrow. Since they didn't have school right now, she would love their company. They could swim while she cooled off in the water without getting her head wet.

Squeals of delight from the girls settled the matter. With a heartfelt thank-you, Soraya ushered her children out of the room.

To Jillian's surprise she felt sleepy. Although the temperature was pleasant inside the casa, she decided that being out in the heat had gotten to her. A little nap wouldn't hurt.

After she awoke, she worked on some ideas, then walked through the house to the kitchen for dinner. Since the men were working late, the three women and the girls gathered for the evening meal. Still later she went back to her room to e-mail Dave and Angela.

She was on the verge of sending it when there was a knock on the door. Thinking it was the girls, she told them to come in.

"*Buenas tardes*, Jillian."

"Remi…" She started to get up, but he told her stay put.

Why was it that every time she saw him after separation, her heart fluttered.

He lounged in the entry with his broad shoulder resting against the doorjamb. Patches of sweat had moistened his shirt. Obviously he'd just come in from a hard day's work. She could see the darker shadow on his jaw. As far as she was concerned, he'd never looked more attractive.

"I understand you'd like to go on a carriage ride." Jillian shouldn't have been surprised word traveled so fast. "Will tomorrow evening be soon enough for you?"

"Only if it won't be an inconvenience."

Remi straightened to his full height. "I could use the distraction." His comment was a reminder of the torturous memories he continually had to suppress in order to survive.

"I'll see you and the girls in the courtyard at seven." On that note he disappeared. She stared at the closed door wondering how she was going to make it through the next twenty-four hours.

Luckily the ideas and drawings she was working on occupied her time. By the next evening she stood near the fountain just as excited as the girls while they waited for the first sight of the carriage. She, of course, was waiting for Remi. Heat from the day still rose from the ground, but having spent several hours with paper and pencil in the mill house, she was getting used to it.

Marcia must have heard the sound of the horses' hooves the second Jillian did. The girl's dark brown eyes flew in her direction. Nina simply jumped up and down clapping her hands.

Jillian exchanged smiles with the women standing a few feet away. According to Maria, the carriage hadn't been brought out since the death of Remi's mother.

Suddenly a beautifully matched team of white horses with black spots appeared. They were pulling the black carriage that rounded the side of the main house. Jillian's gasp coincided with the girls', who'd never experienced this particular adventure before. Elaborate leather trappings with red tassels and bells covered the horses' heads and bodies. To everyone's delight the horses' movements caused them to sway, bob and jangle.

Soraya's husband Miguel sat next to Remi, who held the reins. Paco rode in the carriage. Exhilaration spiraled through Jillian. It was a surreal moment for her. After a year of mourning Kyle, she realized she'd put the pain behind her.

For the first time since his death she felt alive. Really alive.

As Remi drove the horses closer to them, his penetrating black gaze found hers. The collision sent her into shock much as a bolt of lightning would have done.

Paco got out and helped his grandchildren to climb in. Maria and Soraya followed. Jillian took pictures before getting in last. She was glad she'd chosen to wear her white cargo pants and green silk blouse. This way she didn't have to worry about the hem of a dress or skirt riding up her legs like it had done the other day in front of Remi. She took her place next to Nina and her mother.

"Everyone in?" Remi looked over his shoulder. Jillian couldn't take her eyes off him. It didn't matter that he was dressed in his white workshirt and jeans like the men. He stood out. The process of natural selection had decreed it.

"Vamos!" Paco called out.

The next few hours were ones Jillian would always remember. Remi drove the horses to some groves where the oldest olive trees grew on the property. Their height and girth were noticeably bigger than the trees she'd seen the other day. Every day on the estate contributed to her education, causing her to clamor for more.

Tonight the festive atmosphere Remi had created prompted the little girls to sing. As the sun was sinking below the horizon, everyone joined in. Jillian didn't know the songs, which was just as well since she sang off-key, but she enjoyed listening to Remi's sensuous baritone voice. In fact she didn't want the outing to end. Neither did the children, who were vocal about it once they started to head back.

That special feel of family togetherness was something she hadn't experienced for a long time. She expressed as much to Remi after they'd reached the courtyard and she'd climbed out of the carriage.

His dark eyes slanted down at her. "I'm glad you enjoyed it."

High up in the driver's seat with his wavy black hair and burnished complexion, he didn't know how attractive he looked. He was the epitome of male strength and Spanish pride. It hurt to look at him.

"I'll never forget anything about my time here," her voice throbbed. She took one more picture, hoping there was still enough light to capture this moment.

"*Gracias*, Remi!" the children shouted.

A slash of a gleaming white smile in that handsome bronzed face showed briefly before he drove the carriage out of the courtyard with the other men.

Jillian knew it would take him a while to put the carriage back in the barn and see to the horses. Since he had to be up at dawn, she realized she would have another long wait until she saw him again tomorrow evening, *if* then. Because he lived in the house to the north of the casa, she didn't have the hope of seeing him going and coming.

Had he and his wife lived in the main house until his world came crashing down?

She hadn't dared ask those questions, but whatever the answer, the long hours he worked and the distance he kept from Jillian guaranteed there'd been little contact with him since leaving the hospital.

Much as she dreaded what she would find out at the doctor's office, she was looking forward to the drive, where she would have Remi's undivided attention.

It wasn't just because she couldn't wait to share her ideas with him. The unvarnished truth was, she craved his presence. When he rounded a corner or came into a room, he charged the atmosphere with his own brand of electricity. She felt the buzz from the soles of her feet to the last hair on her head.

Until Remi drove her to the Prado Inn after the visit with Dr. Filartigua, she wouldn't dwell on what it was going to be like to watch him walk away. Of course if it worked out that her company would be doing business with him, it followed she would have further conversations with him by phone or the Internet, but she'd no longer be a guest in his home. She wouldn't have access to him in the same way. The intimacy they'd shared in the hospital was one of those moments out of time she'd never experience again.

No matter what she had to do, she couldn't let him know how devastated she would be to get on with her life without him. During the night she'd had to face the painful truth that he wouldn't suffer any loss to leave her because it wasn't a question of his being interested in her. How could he be?

One didn't recover from what he'd been through and still have faith to get involved in another romantic relationship. That wouldn't be happening to him, let alone with her.

Maybe years down the road his loneliness would cause him to reach out to a local woman for companionship, but he'd never be able to summon the kind of love and passion he'd once felt for the woman who'd betrayed him.

Jillian shouldn't be feeling heartache over that sobering fact. Unfortunately she *did* feel it because she was hopelessly in love with Remi.

Having known love before, she recognized all the signs, but this time everything was different. With Kyle there'd been no obstacles, no baggage for either of them. Their happy future lay before them. In Remi's case she was doomed to love him from a distance without his ever knowing about it.

Like a bird thinking a window was open, she could fly to him but she would crash against the invisible glass protecting what was left of his wounded soul. A shard of glass had already damaged her eye. She couldn't afford a broken neck, too.

So she would have to love him from a distance and feel joy knowing their chance meeting had resulted in him finding a new way to keep his heritage safe in an uncertain future. Tonight's tour of the olive groves had infected her with pride in the Goyo name and what it stood for. Any tourists fortunate enough to stop here would go away having been given a figurative as well as literal taste of the glory of Castile's past.

CHAPTER SIX

REMI NOTICED Dr. Filartigua's reception room was filled with patients wearing eye patches. Apparently this was the post-operative day for his cataract patients, all of them much older than Jillian. The nurse called them back every five minutes for a quick check.

He'd driven Jillian to Madrid early that morning to make certain she was on time for her appointment. As it turned out they were early. He guided her to the only empty chair and remained standing until the room started to empty.

Looking fresh and incredibly attractive in a peach-colored sundress with its charming little short-sleeved jacket, she drew everyone's attention. While she waited to know the extent of the damage to her eye, no one would know the depth of her fear. Remi was the one exception.

During the drive from the estate he'd been treated to her heightened animation and conversation. Her remodeling ideas were brilliant, but he could hardly concentrate because he knew all that emotion covered anxieties building since the accident.

When she'd met him outside the main house at eight this morning she'd been carrying her suitcase. His first instinct was to take it from her and put it back in the house, but he didn't act on it. Jillian had been bracing herself for today and didn't need anything to upset her.

Without saying a word he'd stowed the suitcase in the trunk of his car. He'd wait until they left the doctor's office before further discussion about her future took place.

"Senora Gray? Come with me, please."

The reception area had emptied. It was Jillian's turn. Whether she wanted him or not, Remi followed her back to the last room. While the nurse helped her to sit on the end of the examining table, he found a chair and sat down.

"Dr. Filartigua will be right in."

As soon as she went out the door, Jillian darted him a glance. "This is it." Relief filled his system that her first words hadn't told him she wanted to be alone. "Did I tell you I couldn't see anything the last time I put in the drops?"

She'd prepared herself for the worst, but no one was truly ready to hear bad news, least of all Remi. If he hadn't been on the highway at that moment, he doubted the accident would have happened. Regardless, he had to be strong for her now.

"That was four days ago. A lot of healing has gone on since then."

He heard her take in a deep breath. "Whatever happens, thank you for seeing me through this."

"Where else would I be?"

"At work."

"Not today." Before he could say more, the door opened and the doctor walked in. "Senora Gray. Has it been a week already?" He nodded to Remi.

"How are you, Doctor?" She sounded casual. Her courage would always humble Remi.

"I'll know when I've removed this and learn what's going on in there. Lift your head a little higher." She did his bidding.

Adrenaline drove Remi to his feet. He watched the doctor remove the tape and peel the patch away.

"Oh!" she cried out at once. "I can see!"

Remi's body quivered in reaction. Those first joyous words were the sweetest he'd ever known.

"That's fine," the doctor murmured. "How much can you see?"

"It's blurry in the center, but the sides are perfect!"

"How blurry?"

"Um, like a piece of wadded-up cellophane."

The doctor nodded, then got up to turn off the overhead light. "All right," he said, coming back, "let me take a look inside." He moved the eye equipment around and told her to fit her chin into the groove for the exam. "Look straight ahead and try not to blink."

As she cooperated and followed his subsequent directions, Remi held his breath, waiting for a final verdict.

Finally the exam was over. The doctor pulled the machine away and turned on the light.

"Will the blurriness clear up?" she asked in a hopeful voice. Remi wanted the answer to the same question.

Dr. Filartigua walked over to her, cocking his head. "The hazy part of your field of vision will remain permanent."

Permanent…

A groan rose in Remi's throat.

"You have a condition called corneal scotoma. In lay terms it's the blind spot left by the shard that went through to the retina."

"I see."

"In time you'll adjust to the impairment. If the Conde hadn't acted as quickly as he did, the internal bleeding could have affected the whole eye. Frankly, I didn't think your peripheral vision would be saved. That means your right eye won't be as dominant. It's a great plus ." He patted her shoulder kindly.

"It is," she whispered. "Thank you for saving what you could, Doctor."

"You're welcome, Senora. You only need to wear the patch at night to protect the eye while you sleep. Continue the drops from the purple label twice a day for three more weeks, then I want to see you again."

After a silence, she asked, "Can I wash my hair yet?"

While Remi smiled through his unshed tears, the doctor chuckled. "If someone else does it for you. In three weeks you can return to your normal life and no more patch. On your way out, make an appointment with the receptionist."

She nodded.

Remi shook the doctor's hand, then turned to Jillian to help her down off the examining table, but when her feet touched the floor he found he couldn't let her go.

Pulling her closer, he buried his lips in her hair. "You're the bravest woman I've ever known. *Gracias al cielo* you're still able to see something out of that eye."

Her hands slid up his chest beneath his suit jacket. The sensation felt like liquid fire. "If it hadn't been for you…" She rose on tiptoe and softly kissed his lips. "Thank you, dearest Remi."

It wasn't enough. He wanted to really kiss her, but she eased away from him too fast.

"We need to get going." She reached for her patch and put it in her handbag. "You have a long drive back to the estate."

He chose to keep silent a little longer and followed her out the door. At the desk she made an appointment. The receptionist gave her a pair of throwaway sunglasses. "Use these if the light is too bright."

"Thank you."

Remi noticed she didn't put them on. He cupped her elbow and ushered her down the hall to the doors, but the moment they stepped outside, she halted. His arm went around her waist, fearing she felt faint. "What's wrong?"

"N-nothing," she stammered. "I'm sorry if I alarmed you. But without the patch it's like seeing everything in Technicolor after being used to black and white."

"I'm sure it will take some getting used to." She nodded and put the sunglasses on.

"Better?" he murmured near her ear.

"Much." She let out a little laugh. "Ironic isn't it, when I've been praying to see anything at all? You don't realize what your eye takes in until it can't."

Her comment reached right into his heart. He squeezed her waist before removing his hand. They walked to the parking lot at the side of the building and he helped her into his car.

Once behind the wheel he turned to her. "I know you want to phone your brother and tell him the good news, but before you do, I've a favor to ask."

Her head was bowed. "After what you've done for me, how could I refuse?"

He stared at her appealing profile. "Stay at the estate until your next appointment."

"I—I couldn't do that."

Her breathing sounded shallow. Why?

"You've done too much for me already," she added.

"You haven't heard me out."

"Sorry." She kneaded her hands nervously. "Please finish what you were going to say."

"Your ideas for the remodeling are outstanding. Since you can't go back to being a tour guide yet, I'd like you to talk over our business idea with a building contractor I've contacted. With you on the site he'll be able to capture your vision."

Her head jerked in his direction, causing the ends of her silky gold hair to swish against her shoulders. Both eyes stared incredulously at him through the sunglasses. With or without them, she took his breath.

"I have a lot of work to do right now and can't be around that often," he went on to say. "It will relieve my mind to know you're overseeing a project that has the potential to make money for both of us. I'm relying on you."

Maybe if he could get her involved enough, she might even forget to miss her deceased husband for segments of the day. Remi wasn't fool enough to believe that because she never talked about him, he wasn't continually on her mind.

When he'd felt her hands on his chest a few minutes ago, he'd feared she'd been wishing he were her husband and just for a split moment he wished he was. The thought was like a punch in the gut.

When Remi had fallen for his wife, he'd thought no man had ever loved more completely. After she and Javier had betrayed him, he'd thought he'd died and would never come back to life. Yet no one was more surprised than Remi, who sat here waiting for Jillian's answer with more fear and trembling than he cared to admit.

He didn't even need to look at the woman sitting next to him to realize such definitive statements like *never* or *ever* had a brief shelf life.

Jillian struggled to contain her emotions. Had he really asked her to stay at the casa until her next appointment? She knew he didn't need her in order to go ahead with the remodeling. So what *did* it mean?

She knew what she *wanted* it to mean, but she'd only be fooling herself if she thought he had a personal interest in her.

There was only one explanation. Jillian had sought him out with a proposal on behalf of her tour company. Because of the complicated circumstances of the accident, they'd been thrown together and he'd discovered her idea had merit. After having been betrayed by those he'd loved most, it was only natural he'd prefer to work with her instead of a stranger. It was a miracle he trusted *her*.

Trying to keep the excitement out of her voice she said, "Thank you for your generosity, Remi. I *would* like to be on hand to see the changes, so I'll take you up on your offer on one condition."

"Name it." She thought he sounded pleased and possibly relieved. After all, he was already planning on supplementing his income with her idea.

"When the contractor doesn't need me, let me help around the casa or elsewhere. Dr. Filartigua was right. I *am* a workaholic, so please find something for me to do. That way I won't feel like I'm always taking from you."

"Agreed. What do you think you'd like to do?"

"Anything! Just point me in a direction."

He chuckled. It was a glorious sound, one she'd rarely heard come out of him. "Let's celebrate with lunch before we head back. Have you ever eaten at the Taberna Los Cabales? It's on the south side of the Plaza de Santa Ana."

"No. The few times one of our tours has come to Madrid, we've eaten at the Zalacain."

"That's a good restaurant for big crowds. The Taberna is much cozier and they serve excellent tapas."

It thrilled her to be with him no matter what they did. "I'd love to try it."

He flicked her a penetrating glance that sent feathery sensations through her body. "Better fasten your seat belt." With that suggestion he started the engine.

"Imagine forgetting that after it saved my life—" She did it quickly. "I'd better call my brother." Jillian was all thumbs opening her purse.

"I'm sure he's waiting."

While they pulled out of the parking lot, she rang Dave, who picked up before the second ring. "Jilly?" he cried her name anxiously. The love she felt from him caused her eyes to smart.

"I have terrific news, brother dear! I can see out of my eye. There's one little spot that's blurry and will stay that way, but everything else is perfect. I've been so blessed."

The doctor wasn't kidding when he'd said it would take a while to get used to partial vision, but Jillian wasn't going to complain.

Too overcome with emotion, Dave didn't say anything for a second. Taking advantage of the quiet she said, "I wish I could talk longer but another patient is waiting outside the examining room. Go back to sleep. I'll call you tonight. 'Bye for now. Love you."

Remi couldn't have helped overhear her tell that little fib about still being in the doctor's office. He could make of it what he liked. After everything he'd done for her, it would hurt him if he knew how Dave felt. Remi had received enough hurts to last a lifetime. She'd do anything to protect him.

As they drove along she noticed that all the eating establishments were filled, yet Remi managed to get a table on the sidewalk of the Taberna. After they were seated opposite each other at one of the charming bistro tables, a waiter handed them menus and took their wine order.

She shook her head at Remi. "Not this early in the day for

me. Especially when I couldn't manage breakfast this morning. What I'd like is a tall glass of orange juice."

"I didn't eat, either," he confessed *sotto voce* as if they were conspirators. He looked at the waiter. "Make that two large orange juices and a tray of assorted tapas."

The other man nodded and disappeared inside the crowded restaurant. Jillian had a hunch Remi had decided against wine because of the drive ahead of them after lunch, but he always said and did the thing that would make her the most comfortable.

She loved him for it. She loved *him*. It was a good thing her sunglasses were on. Eyes conveyed emotions like nothing else. She preferred to hide hers and look into his while he wasn't aware of it. They were inky black, yet they could brood, darken in pain, lighten in amusement, blaze in fury or pierce to the quick. How did that work?

"What have you decided?" His deep voice penetrated the sudden silence between them.

Her cheeks went hot. He'd caught her staring after all. She had to think fast. "This is the first time I've had a chance to really look at you out of both eyes."

He sat back in the chair. With his black hair she found him devilishly striking dressed in a light gray summer suit. He'd toned it with a darker gray button-down shirt he'd left open at the neck. "Do I terrify you?"

She smiled. Yes, he terrified her because of the desire he'd aroused in her. It interfered with her breathing. "I haven't run away yet, have I?" she teased to cover this onslaught of emotions she was having difficulty keeping under control.

While she waited for him to say something, the waiter chose that moment to serve them. It was just as well she didn't hear Remi's reply. Her gaze fastened on the dozen or so hors d'oeuvres arranged on an enormous platter. There was hardly room for their own plates. Next came the juice.

"*Que aproveche!*" he bid them before moving to another table.

"Try this first." Remi used what looked like a cake server to put one on her plate. "This one's called *pil-pil.*" An amusing name. The strong smell of garlic reached her nostrils. "It's smoked cod cooked in its own sauce with olive oil."

Jillian dug in and couldn't stop with just one. Next came smoked salmon, then herb-flavored shrimps called *gambas* followed by crabmeat *cangrejos* with potato tortillas.

"It's a good thing I'm not staying in Madrid for the next three weeks. In that amount of time I'd easily put on ten pounds eating here every day." She'd never tasted anything so good. In fact it gave her an idea, but she didn't have the temerity to share her thoughts with him just yet.

"I can sense there's something on your mind, Jillian. Like to tell me what it is?"

He had the uncanny ability to read her mood and wouldn't let go until he'd unearthed answers. She'd have to be very careful he couldn't read her personal thoughts about him.

"These tapas," she began. "I bet Maria would know how to make all of them and teach me."

"Sí." She had his full attention.

"I'm thinking big now, but it's just an idea so don't be too upset with me."

"How big?"

"Big. The whole time we've been eating lunch I've had this vision."

He rubbed his hard jaw with his palm. "I hear dollar signs. Is it going to break the bank?"

She fidgeted with her purse. "Temporarily maybe."

"Maybe?" he asked silkily.

"Probably, but it's a fabulous idea. You have an authentic setting on your property for something so unique and incredible, I've got goose bumps."

"You've got the hair standing on the back of my neck. Go on."

"What if you made the mill house into a tapas bar that would be open to the public as well as the tour bus groups? It would become the most famous tapas bar in all Spain. You could call it Holy Toledo!"

His dark head went back and deep laughter rumbled out of him, causing heads to turn.

She laughed, too. "It's an old expression Americans say when they're stupefied by something extraordinary. Considering you live so close to Toledo, I think it fits."

Once he'd recovered, he asked in a deadpan voice, "Is there anything else you haven't told me about this vision?"

"Well, as a matter of fact I was thinking you could provide entertainment on the weekends. That floor in the barn was made for flamenco dancing and those who wanted could take a carriage ride.

"What makes it so nice is that you could open up the old gate farther down the highway, the one you told me about that was closed off a long time ago. Using that entrance to the property would ensure people's access to the bar without coming near your own private living quarters."

He didn't interrupt her. It prompted her to rush on.

"The olive press house could be a store to sell your fabulous product on demand. You could have little recipe books printed to tell how the tapas are made with Soleado Goyo olive oil. Yours would be the showplace of Castile-La Mancha."

He was quiet too long as she knew he would be. "Like I

said, I was thinking big." She put her napkin down. "I'm ready to leave when you are."

His dark eyebrows lifted in query. "Am I to assume you don't want dessert?"

"After orange juice, I couldn't."

"Maybe I can change your mind." With that cryptic comment, he put some bills on the table. "Shall we go?"

The female eyes fastened on him were legion, but he seemed oblivious. She liked the feeling of possession as he guided her through the tables to a crowded pastry shop near the end of the plaza.

It was a mistake to go in. While she was salivating over everything in sight, he bought two fabulous-looking treats for them. His dark gaze found hers. "I know you have marzipan in the States, but you've never tasted it like they make it here."

"In that case let's get enough for everyone at the casa. I'd like it to be my contribution."

He didn't interfere as she opened her purse and pulled out enough euros to pay for six more.

After thanking the saleswoman she turned to Remi, who was already eating his and insisted she try it. He put it to her lips. With her purse in one hand and the sack of pastries in the other, he'd left her no choice but to take a bite.

His fingers brushed against her lips, making her lightheaded with longing. "No more, Remi," she cried, laughing and endeavoring to swallow at the same time. By his dashing grin, he was obviously enjoying himself. So was she. Too much.

For the first time since the accident she was beginning to understand her brother's concern. He wasn't nearly as worried about Remi as he was Jillian's willingness to be the guest of a man with the Senor's importance and background.

More than Remi's motives, it was *her* heart Dave was worried about.

My dear brother…if only you knew it was too late for warnings. Seven days too late.

She started to follow Remi out the door, but he suddenly stopped dead in his tracks. It came without warning, causing her to bump into him. The sack dropped from her hand.

Jillian reached down for it, then looked up to see another man right outside the shop who bore a faint resemblance to Remi. The other man's lean body stood frozen in place. Even with her sunglasses on, she could tell the color had drained from his face.

"Javier," Remi said, acknowledging him.

Her chest felt this stabbing pain before Remi's hand closed around her wrist. He had no idea of his strength, but she didn't cry out. Together they left the shop, sweeping past his brother to find the car parked around the corner.

After helping her in, his long, powerful length slid behind the wheel. He sat there without turning on the ignition. Wanting only to comfort him, she reached across the seat and covered the top of his hand welded to the gearshift.

Jillian had no idea how much time went by before Remi drew her hand to his mouth and kissed the palm. Weakness attacked her body. When he finally relinquished it, they left the city without speaking. Once out on the highway she sensed him stir.

CHAPTER SEVEN

"YOU'VE STARTED ME thinking big, Senora Gray." His first words since they'd left the shop.

She angled her head toward him. Relieved and thankful he'd survived one of those black moments in life he hadn't seen coming she said, "How big?"

"If I were to go along with most of your suggestions, would you be willing to ask for a sabbatical until the harvest begins?"

Her pulse hammered in her throat. *He wanted her to stay on the estate until December?*

Fighting to keep the tremor out of her voice she said, "To do what?"

"Run the tapas bar and the gift shop. You had me going back at the Taberna. I've done some research on EuropaUltimate Tours. Their tour guides come highly recommended. Mr. Santorelli sang your praises."

"When did you speak to him?" she cried in surprise.

"Yesterday."

She couldn't keep up with Remi. "He hardly knows me!"

"A CEO worth his salt will have made a thorough study of the employees in his company. He and your immediate boss, Pia Richter, couldn't say enough in your favor."

So he'd been in touch with Pia, too. The head of Jillian's

division hadn't mentioned talking to Remi. "They probably feel sorry for me and were just being diplomatic," she whispered.

"It isn't every day someone has an accident like yours. As for your sterling six-year employment record, that speaks for itself," he added in a faintly husky tone. "I can tell you right now they won't be happy if you ask for a leave of absence from your guide duties."

Jillian was too dazed by his offer to answer him.

He darted her a measuring glance. "With your flair for dealing with people and your ability to carry on conversation in a variety of languages, you'd be a natural to front our project. Instead of riding the bus with your flock for days on end, you could concentrate your efforts here."

She clasped her hands together. "Now you're frightening me."

"How so? After all, it *is* your brainchild. By December we should have some idea if the project is a solid one."

"I—I don't know if I could do it," she stammered. To stay on the estate that long would throw them into each other's company every day. *And night.* She would never want to leave him then. She didn't now…

"With you in charge we'll increase our chances of success, but maybe the thought of not traveling around the continent makes you stir-crazy. You and your husband enjoyed married life on the move." There was a slight pause before he said, "If it's in your blood, I'd be the last person to try to keep you here."

He had to be speaking about his ex-wife. Jillian wasn't anything like her and couldn't allow him to continue with his faulty assumption.

"That's not why I'm reticent, Remi."

She heard his harsh intake of breath. "Then it means you can't see as well out of that eye as you've been pretending."

He was still feeling guilty about the accident! She couldn't bear to hear the self-recrimination in his voice.

"No, Remi—"

"'No what'?" he answered right back.

"You don't understand." She shook her head. "When you first heard my proposal, you were thinking of adding some bathrooms and remodeling one of the buildings to supply a cold drink for the tourists. But then I threw in my big ideas, forgetting you have to come up with the extra money." She paused. "I just wouldn't want anything to go wrong for you…." Her voice trailed shakily. "You've been through enough."

"So what you're saying is, you're worried about *me*."

She studied her nails. "Naturally I am."

"Then why not stay on the estate and help me. With an experiment like this, two heads are better than one." His compelling argument trumped her deepest fear. If he had any idea how much she loved him, he'd turn the car around and head back to Madrid.

"Tell you what. When we reach the estate I'll e-mail Pia. Provided she's all right with it, I'll do everything I can to make this project a success."

"Then it's guaranteed," he said on a note of satisfaction. With those words her fate was sealed no matter what the future held for her personally.

Jillian was too crazy about Remi to think of leaving him yet. Never—if she had her way.

She felt his glance on her. "You've gone quiet on me. Don't be afraid to take a nap. Today hasn't been like any other day."

"Not for you, either," she murmured, but he heard her.

"Don't worry. Since my brother sold his part of the olive groves, I've run into him several times on my trips to Toledo."

Jillian let out a gasp. "He sold them?" She shook her head. "How could he have done such a thing?"

"I'm sure I don't know."

From the expression she'd seen on Javier's face, she'd had the strongest feeling he was filled with remorse. His eyes seemed to have been begging Remi. For what exactly? Forgiveness? A chance to talk?

She hadn't thought she could be more shocked, but it wasn't true. And what of Remi's ex-wife? Where was she? Had she tried to come back? Questions riddled Jillian, but Remi wasn't supplying answers. Why would he when it was none of her business.

"Who owns it now?"

"A vulture who's been hoping Soleado Goyo would go into receivership. One day in the future I plan to buy the land back."

"Were your inheritances equal?"

"Sí. He still owns the house to the south of the courtyard. Two years ago I asked Soraya and her family to move in there to keep it up until Javier decides what he's going to do with it."

Aghast she cried, "So you lost half an income along with the brother who helped you run everything?"

"It's all right. In two years I've been able to pay off the rest of the loan our father took out years ago."

She clutched the armrests. "I can't let you take out a new one! I *won't* let you."

"The money's minimal and I've already seen to the arrangements. Though he didn't realize it at the time, my father made the wrong business decision. We paid a heavy price, but this venture isn't the same thing."

Jillian stared hard at him. "How do you dare put yourself at risk again?"

"For one thing I now have *you* for a business partner."

"But I haven't proven myself yet."

His fierce eyes glittered. "Do you honestly think we'd be having this conversation if I didn't have faith in you?"

"That's very flattering," she said, her voice shaking.

"Have you forgotten the drought could last several more years? I'm already at risk. Fortunately the enterprise you and I've entered into isn't affected by the weather to keep it going. We can depend on a certain amount of tourist traffic year-round barring terrorist attacks at the airports worldwide or all-out global war," he said.

"Heaven forbid," she muttered.

He chuckled. "If that happens we're all doomed anyway. In the meantime I'd like your ideas about advertising for drop-in customers."

She gave him a half smile. "Are we talking about the Holy Toledo?" They'd just passed the city in question and would be back on the estate shortly.

"I don't see why not. Even if the Americans are the only ones who get the point, the association with Toledo will be enough to make a lasting impression on tourists of other nationalities. Especially *my* countrymen. We Goyos are descendents of one of the Dukes of Toledo."

"You're kidding." She hid her head in her hands. "I had no idea. Your ancestors would probably turn over in their graves."

"Undoubtedly. That's why I'm so taken with your suggestion."

"Dangerous *and* irreverent, too," she quipped daringly, producing a laugh from him.

He really liked her idea. She could feel it. "I'm getting excited, Remi."

"So am I," he said in his deep, vibrant voice, "and that hasn't happened in a long time."

"I know what you mean." But she wasn't talking about business. Clearing her throat, she said, "The tour bus crowds will be the best source of advertising, but to get things started we could promote the grand opening in the newspaper."

Peeking at him out of her good eye she said, "I looked up your Web site on the Internet. We could make an announcement there. I'll work up a flier to place at the local tourist agencies in Toledo and Madrid. Being a tour guide, I know some of the people. They'll distribute them for us. If we have a good turnout, word of mouth will do the rest."

He reached for her hand.

When he'd held it in the hospital, it had been to comfort her. In the pastry shop he'd grasped her wrist for support. This time his strong fingers twined with hers, sending out a different message, one she was afraid to read for fear she would interpret it wrong.

At a glance their joined hands reminded her of the other evening while they'd taken the carriage ride around a portion of the property. In one of the groves the trees had been planted in pairs almost like they were lovers. The odd notion had jumped into her mind then and wouldn't leave.

When she'd asked Remi about it, he'd drawn the horses to a stop and had turned in the seat to explain. As he spoke to her, the slanting rays of the sun bathed his arresting features, causing his eyes to look slumberous.

"We call these trees cultivars. Since this type is self-sterile or nearly so, we plant them in pairs with a single primary cultivar and a secondary cultivar selected for its ability to fertilize the primary one."

He'd supplied the answer and she'd been shaken by it.

That odd notion was still in her mind, only now it had taken root in her heart.

Remi didn't let go until they drove through the gate. After parking the car, he carried her suitcase into the *casa* and put it down inside the bedroom. "Meet me in the patio room in fifteen minutes. We'll soak in the pool and plot."

The glint in those black eyes rocked her to her foundation.

Remi waited in the water for Jillian. They were alone in the house for the first time. Paco was at the plant. Maria and the others had gone to the nearest village of Arges to do some shopping. She'd left food prepared, but after the meal he and Jillian had enjoyed in Madrid, he doubted his guest was hungry yet.

Fifteen minutes turned into twenty-five. He had half a mind to walk back to the bedroom and knock on her door. Just as he started to get out of the pool, she came out on the patio with those long elegant legs exposed carrying a towel over her arm. A thigh-length beach coat in small green and white stripes covered up the suit he couldn't see. The sunglasses had been removed. Now he could look into her eyes.

His pulse rate picked up. He swam the length of the pool, but didn't get out. "Before we do anything else, let's wash your hair." He lifted a bottle of shampoo he'd brought out with his towel. In the hospital he'd noticed she liked strawberry so he'd purchased something similar.

She looked stunned. "You mean here?"

His mouth quirked. "This isn't a natural swimming pool. It's fresh water, no chlorine. A few suds aren't going to hurt anything. Put your towel down by mine and lie on it with your head hanging over the edge. I'll support you."

He sensed her reluctance.

"Didn't your husband ever wash your hair for you?" Remi held her gaze until she murmured yes.

"I promise not one drop of water will get in your eyes."

She still seemed hesitant. "Did I just imagine you asking the doctor how soon you could have a shampooing?"

She shook her head.

I can wait as long as you can, Senora.

Another few seconds and she arranged the towel on the tiles next to his. Without removing her modest cover-up, she sat down and lay back, inching her body until he could cup her well-shaped head in his palm.

With his other hand he poured the cool water over her hair, careful to protect her beyond her hairline.

"Oh…" Her sigh invaded his body.

"You like that?" he whispered.

"You can't imagine."

Yes, he could. He leaned over her. The lines of her generous, heart-shaped mouth mesmerized him. She had a widow's peak, too, and shell-like ears. Most women had pierced lobes, but hers were as smooth as petals and her roots were pure gold like the ends of her hair.

From this angle, with the light shining between the lattice-work, he saw something he hadn't noticed before. The surgery had changed the configuration of her pupil. It now resembled a pear. Had she already seen it and suffered in silence because that part of her eye would never be restored? His gut clenched.

Jillian…

He felt his eyelids prickle and had to will himself to stop trembling before getting on with the task.

Once he'd steeled back his emotions, he poured some shampoo onto her golden mass of hair and began to massage her scalp. Slowly he covered every inch, all the while breathing in the fruit-scented fragrance. Her skin exuded warmth. He could feel every breath she took.

As he worked up a lather, his senses filled until his body grew heavy with longing for this woman who was still in mourning for her husband. Remi had no right to touch her except like this. He would drag it out as long as she would let him.

"You have magic in your fingers, *Senor*."

"When we pick the olives, we have to treat them like newborn babies."

Her lips curved. "One day when you have your own babies, they'll be lucky to have you for their father."

His hands stilled in her hair. "You think?"

"I *know*. I've been the recipient of your strength and tenderness when I needed help most. Maybe it comes from working with the gift from the gods. I read that Homer called olive oil 'liquid gold'."

"That's what it is," Remi mused aloud, studying the golden strands he swirled in his fingers.

"I want to watch you make it."

He liked the sound of that. "Next week I'll walk you through the process. Then you can decide which parts will be of interest to the tourists."

"I'm sure every aspect will be utterly fascinating."

Her enthusiasm made him see everything through new eyes. No matter what life threw at her, she was a woman who embraced it head-on. Being in her company imbued him with an excitement he'd never experienced before. Not like this.

Smothering a groan because this erotic experience had to come to an end, he began to rinse out the suds, but he took his time.

"How does that feel?" he said at last, giving her one last rinse.

She reached behind her head and pulled on one of the strands, trying to break the tension hanging thick in the air. "Hear that?" she laughed softly. "I'm squeaky clean for the first time in over a week. What luxury."

He squeezed as much water as he could out of her hair. "Now hold still while I get you dry."

Remi reached for his towel and wrapped it turban style around her head, making sure no water dripped down her forehead. "Go ahead and sit up."

While she did his bidding he levered himself out of the pool onto the tiles. "Let me help." He held out his hand and pulled her to her feet before letting go. Maybe he was mistaken, but he thought she was trembling. Then again he was so affected by her nearness, it could have been him.

He thrust his hand through his damp hair in frustration, wondering how she would react if he suggested they both get back in the pool and let the cool water lap against their bodies. This ache for her was so real it was driving him out of his mind.

She sat down in the nearest chair to finish drying her hair, then she looked up at him. "Tell me what I can do to repay you."

Remi thought she sounded way too composed after what he'd just experienced touching her like that. He sank down in the other chair. "You already have. Today you agreed to be my business partner, pending your company's willingness to give you a leave of absence." Her brother was another matter but he'd think about that later. "I've been operating for a long time without one."

"That won't be a problem. Pia already told me to take all the time I need before coming back. At this point it's just a formality to tell her."

"Then I'm relieved." *Just keep on talking, Goyo, before you give yourself away and grab her.* Taking a deep breath he said, "How long do your tour groups usually stop at a vineyard?"

"Two hours from start to finish."

"That sounds doable here."

"I don't know. Once they start eating Soleado Goyo tapas, we'll never be able to get rid of them. I'll build the cost of soft drinks into the itinerary price. Food and wine will be extra. We'll make them pay cash." He heard the satisfaction in her voice. "You'll bring in a small fortune on that alone."

"With your business savvy, I don't doubt it." Apparently business was the only thing on her mind, or was it? She was a deep one.

"I think we should get some postcards made up showing the mill house and the olive press house with the groves in the background. We'll sell them in the store. It's another great way to advertise and keep the cost down. Once we've set our budget, I promise we won't go over it. What do you think?"

I can't take sitting next to you without touching you.

"I think we have our work cut out for us."

"We do. One of the things we haven't talked about is the furniture for the bar. If it held a maximum of sixty people, then we'd need maybe eight large, round tables that could seat eight, but bistro size would be more charming."

"We have a couple of old refectory tables and matching armoires that haven't seen use in years."

She let out a happy sound. "How old are they?"

"Seventeenth century. Cherry wood with lyre-styled legs."

Another squeal came out of her. "Are they very long?"

"They can seat sixteen each."

"Oh, Remi…if we had benches built on either side of the entry, we could put the tables there and have room for all the chairs and bistro tables."

Jillian had no idea how tempting she looked with her golden hair in sensual disarray.

"I'll rummage up our old coat of arms. It used to hang in the foyer, but my mother thought it made the house feel like a fortress so it's stored upstairs. In fact there's a lot of furniture we could bring down including a deacon's chair."

"When can we look at everything?"

"I'll tell Maria to show you around any time you'd like."

"You won't be sorry about this, Remi. I'll do it all while you concentrate on running your company. I don't want you to have to worry about a thing."

Where had this woman come from? Eight days ago he hadn't known of her existence. And now…

The urge to take her to bed and make passionate love to her had turned into literal pain because he was forced to deny himself, but she wasn't ready emotionally. He needed to do something fast before he made a mistake that could ruin everything.

"I'll be back with our lunch."

Without waiting for her response he strode to the passageway leading to the kitchen. As he entered it, Paco was coming in through the back door. One look at his face and Remi knew something was wrong.

"I've been trying to reach you on the phone. Eduardo got a deep gash between his thumb and index finger on one of the machines. We stopped the bleeding the best we could. Diego and Juan drove him to the clinic in Arges."

Remi grimaced. First Jillian, now Eduardo. All in one week.

"That means he'll be off the job for a while. I'll go to Arges and check on him, then drive over to their house and assure his wife she doesn't have to worry about expenses his insurance doesn't cover."

Paco nodded. "Shall I call Jorge to fill in tomorrow? He called again this morning asking if we'd consider rehiring him."

"Go ahead. Tell him I'll talk to him about a permanent job after he goes off shift."

Thank heaven Remi had gone to the kitchen. Jillian couldn't have maintained her composure any longer and ran through the house to the bedroom with his towel. Her legs felt as insubstantial as mush.

She'd planned to cool off in the pool, but that was before he'd offered to wash her hair. The need to be touched by him had been so strong she'd willingly put herself in his hands. She would have let him do anything to her just now and she was sure he knew it!

If other people weren't living at La Rosaleda, would he have taken her to the bedroom? Or to his other house? There was a moment out there when he was looking in her eyes, she'd thought he was going to kiss her. She'd stopped breathing while she waited, but something held him back.

He wasn't indifferent to her. She knew that. On some elemental level they had a connection that was growing stronger. She could blame part of his hesitation on the damage done by his ex-wife. After what he'd been through it would take more courage than Jillian had to enter into new relationship, but there was another problem.

She and Remi weren't like ships passing in the night, where they could share a few hours of passion before they both moved on never to see each other again. She couldn't do that anyway. It wasn't how she was made. Kyle had been her only lover, but she wasn't so naive as to suppose Remi hadn't been with other women since his divorce.

This situation was different. They were joined in a financial venture that was vital to both of them. She didn't want anything to go wrong for him and she'd made a commitment to stay until December. To become physically involved would complicate everything.

It already had. Her body still throbbed from his ministrations. What had possessed her out there? For sure she wouldn't be taking any dips in the pool in his presence.

Still shaken by her desire for him, she had to do something to offset it, but how could she do that when she'd be seeing him again in a few minutes? Which reminded her that her hair was a damp mess. She went into the bathroom to brush it into some semblance of order and change into jeans and a T-shirt.

When she emerged a few minutes later, she heard her cell phone ring. Her watch said it was almost four in the afternoon. That would be Dave. He was up by now and wanted to talk before leaving for work. She'd have to call him later. Remi was waiting.

Grabbing the towel off the chair she hurried out of the bedroom to join him. She couldn't reach the patio room fast enough, but all the wind rushed out of her when she discovered he wasn't alone. Her steps slowed.

"*Hola*, Paco."

He nodded with a smile. "Senora." What if the foreman had come in while Remi had been washing her hair? More than ever she realized how careful she needed to be from now on. She laid the towel over the chair.

Her host flicked her a veiled glance. In the interim he'd changed into trousers and a work shirt. She'd give anything to know what he was thinking behind that brooding facade.

"You'll have to excuse me, Jillian. Something urgent has come up that needs my attention. I'll see you later. Enjoy your meal." She watched him leave and felt life go out of the room.

Not wanting to sit here alone, she carried her tray of food back to the bedroom. With unexpected time on her hands she walked over to the laptop and composed an e-mail to Pia while she ate. Once it was sent, she reached for her phone and called her brother.

"Thanks for getting back to me, Jilly. Are you alone?"

Quite alone. She wondered what emergency had called Remi away. "Yes."

"Good. This is your big brother you're talking to now. How bad is it? I want the truth!"

With her emotions in knots over Remi she'd actually forgotten about her eye. She got to her feet and started pacing. "I told you earlier. There's one spot that's blurry. That's it. I'm already used to it."

"No, you're not."

Her hand tightened on the phone. "Listen—there's something more important I have to tell you."

She sank down on the side of the bed. In the next breath she explained about her new business venture and her plan to stay until December.

"Jil—"

"Just hear me out," she interrupted. Having anticipated an argument, she told him about the tragedy Remi had lived through. She hadn't planned on telling him something that private, but the situation had changed drastically since their last conversation.

Her words silenced her brother, who eventually muttered, "The poor devil."

She jumped to her feet, unable to sit still. "He hasn't let it defeat him. Remi's remarkable."

"He sounds like you. But be careful, Jilly. I can hear it in your voice."

Heat filled her cheeks. "Hear what?"

"You're nuts about him. Angela and I've been hoping you'd meet someone, but when a man's been hurt that deeply, those wounds have scarred him. One day he could destroy you without even realizing it. He's not like Kyle in any way, shape or form. You *do* know that."

"Yes," she whispered, trying in vain to hold back the tears.

He made a strange sound in his throat. "I don't think you do, but it's too late for this talk, isn't it?"

The feel of Remi's fingers in her hair still rippled through her body. "I'm afraid it is." She wiped the tears with the back of her free hand. "Let's change the subject. How's Angela doing?"

"All's well. It's the waiting game now."

"Have you picked out a name yet for my newest nephew to be?"

"We've narrowed it down to Max or Matt."

"I like both."

"Maybe our baby won't look like either one and we'll have to come up with something else."

She'd been thinking about Remi's babies, the ones she wanted to have with him. They'd have incredibly long, gorgeous names like Basilio Remigio de Gray y Goyo, or a Carolina Alfonso Domenica de Gray y Goyo. Whether Conde or Condesa, they'd have beautiful olive skin and flashing black eyes. Their children would be loved and cherished and—

"Jilly?"

She blinked. Her brother was still on the line. "I'm here. I was just about to tell you I'll fly over for a quick visit in August to see the new arrival."

"We're all looking forward to that. The kids adore their aunt."

"I love *them*," she said, her voice trembling. "Now I'd better let you go so you can earn your living."

"Don't be upset with me, Jilly. All I want is your happiness."

"That goes both ways. We'll keep in close touch. Love you." She hung up before he could say anything else.

Depending on how things were going by August, maybe Remi would fly over with her. He could visit his distributor in New York. She could drop in to see Pia. They could even write it off as a business expense.

Perhaps Remi would even drive to Albany with her. She wanted the two men in her life to meet. Angela would absolutely die when she saw Senor Goyo for the first time. If Jillian was going to dream, might as well dream big until it all turned into a nightmare.

That was the problem with a wonderful brother like Dave. He'd never steered her wrong. Was she deluding herself to hope the day might come when Remi would reach out for her love?

Troubled by the conversation with Dave, she moved over to the window and looked out through haunted eyes at the olive groves. The blurry spot prevented her from seeing things perfectly. Maybe it went deeper than her eye. Maybe it had impaired her judgment so she only saw what she wanted to see.

Her mind kept replaying what he'd said about Remi. *He's not like Kyle in any way, shape or form.*

No. Her man of La Mancha had demons, and maybe like Don Quixote she would be forever tilting at windmills in an effort to help Remi get past them.

CHAPTER EIGHT

"*GRACIAS.*" The two little girls thanked Jillian for the sack of marzipan she'd bought them in Madrid. She sat with them on the rim of the fountain and ate the delicious confection. This was a favorite spot because there couldn't be a more beautiful courtyard anywhere in Spain.

It was 7:30 p.m. Remi's car was back, but she'd seen no sign of him.

Soraya came out of her house to find her children. They ran over to her with their candy. "The Senora bought these for us!"

Her smiling eyes fell on Jillian. "You spoil them."

"It's my pleasure. They're adorable."

Marcia cocked her head. "Where are your babies?"

"No, Marcia," her mother shushed her with a finger to her lips.

Jillian smiled. "It's all right. I'm not married, but one day I hope to be. There's nothing I'd like more than a couple of little girls as cute as you."

"*Hola*, Remigio." This from Nina.

"*Hola, chicas.*"

Shocked to hear that deep voice, Jillian shifted around to discover him not two feet away. He must have come straight from his house. If he'd been standing there for the last fifteen seconds, he would have heard what she said.

He tousled Marcia's hair before sweeping the younger one in his arms.

"Do you want some marzipan?" Nina handed him a piece from the sack.

"Un million de gracias." He gobbled it in one second, causing the girls to giggle. Jillian laughed quietly. She was no more immune to his potent charm than they were.

"Do you mind if I steal Senora Gray away?" he asked after putting her down with a kiss to her forehead. "We have some business to discuss."

They shook their heads. Soraya reminded them it was past their bedtime. *"Vayamos pasando."*

Jillian thought Remi wanted to talk to her in the main house. Instead he walked over to the car and helped her in the front seat, bracing his hands on both sides of the open door. He smelled and looked so irresistible she needed him to move or she was afraid of crossing a line that could change everything.

"Are you up for another drive?" he asked through veiled eyes. "There's something I want to show you. It's only ten miles round-trip."

Unable to find her voice, she simply nodded.

He shut the door and walked around the car to get behind the wheel. "We have to drive on a dirt road across my property to see it, but it's not rutted so it won't jar you."

She was afraid to look at him. "I don't recall the doctor warning me about driving on a dirt road."

"You wouldn't say that if we were headed into the back country of the Montes de Toledo."

He started the motor and they wound around the side of the main house. In a few minutes he took a road headed in a southeast direction, leaving the cluster of buildings behind.

"Do you camp out up there often?"

"I used to." The hint of melancholy in his voice made her want to weep.

"Do you love it?"

"Sí. What about you?"

"I've never done the kind of camping you're probably talking about, but I always wanted to."

"Living on a high barren flat like this makes me yearn for the occasional trip into the mountains. The Arabs called this area *ma-ansha*, meaning no water. There's nothing so refreshing as cool air to breathe and the sound of rushing water outside your tent during the night."

There'd be nothing comparable to lying in his arms inside the tent. She took a fortifying breath. "How long has it been since you had a real vacation?"

"My honeymoon to the French Riviera."

Her heart did a dropkick. "My husband and I spent our honeymoon there, too. It's a paradise."

"Agreed. Letizia wanted us to move there."

Her eyes rounded. That was the first time he'd mentioned her name. "But she knew you were an olive farmer! How did she expect you to live?"

He gave an elegant shrug of his broad shoulders. "She *didn't* think about it. We met in London while I was there on business. She was tall and stunning-looking. We had a whirlwind affair and married in haste."

Naturally she would have been beautiful. "Are you saying she was British?"

"No. She grew up in Barcelona, but went to work for a company in London with connections to Spain. When I brought her home to the casa, I'm afraid she assumed my resources would allow us to buy a villa she had her eye on in Cap d'Antibes so we could play."

Jillian swallowed hard. She'd seen women like that in her travels. It took all kinds. Some men married them. A few probably lived to regret it. "How old is she?"

Remi leveled a glance on her. "A year older than you, but that's where the similarities end."

She stirred in the seat. For sure Letizia didn't have an eye with a pupil that resembled a misshapen green pepper. For sure his wife didn't have a clue about the man she'd married. Jillian could forgive her for wanting Remi with a mighty passion, but not for anything else.

"D-do you think she still sees your brother?" She'd stumbled over the words getting them out.

"I don't know, and I don't want to know."

She felt that prickly sensation beneath her lids. "I wouldn't want to know, either." After the enormity of what his wife and brother had done to him, anything she said now would come out sounding so trite she was afraid to speak.

The car rolled to a stop. "Take a look out of your side window," he said unexpectedly.

Still haunted by the pain in his voice, she turned in the seat to see what it was he'd driven them out here to show her.

"Windmills!"

There were five of them in the far distance on a little rise. Silhouetted against a twilight sky fast turning into night, she could understand why they were sometimes described as giants. How strange that she'd been thinking about them earlier.

In awe she asked, "Are they on your property?"

"No, but you have to be right here at this exact time of evening to fully appreciate them."

Compelled by the magic of the moment, she undid her seat belt and got out of the car to get a better look. As she stood there mesmerized by the curious brown-and-white structures, a warm breeze arose out of nowhere. Across the undulating landscape it seemed to whisper echoes from past centuries.

While she stayed in place riveted, she felt Remi move behind her. He stood too close. She was on the verge of suffocating from his nearness.

"Was the drive worth it?" The sound of his voice could have been an extension of the elements.

Afraid to look at him she said, "How can you even ask that question?" The silence that followed underlined the frantic pounding of her heart.

"Would you believe during the time we were married, my wife never once came out here to see them?"

Jillian couldn't take any more. "Then she was a *fool!*"

She spun around. Her hands shot out to grasp his upper arms, shaking him a little out of her rage over the woman who'd ripped his heart to shreds. Her moist eyes looked up into his. "She was a fool," Jillian repeated in more hushed tones.

Wanting him to know how wonderful he was, she stretched to reach his lips and sensed his dark head descending. She'd been wanting this for so long that when his mouth covered hers, the breath left her lungs and she found herself falling into him. It felt like the most natural thing in the world to communicate with him like this.

He didn't have to coax her lips apart. She wanted to know his full essence and opened her mouth to him, knowing she was inviting something she might not be able to stop. Later on she'd blush to think about it, but right now she needed him with a desire so fierce it terrified her.

"Remi…" she moaned his name, caught up in ecstasy. She'd known the taste and feel of his mouth would bring her rapture beyond bearing.

The night wind caught at their clothes and disheveled their

hair, but its force couldn't compare to the firestorm he was whipping up inside of her. She couldn't get enough of him. A groan escaped her throat as he molded her body to his. When he ran his strong hands over her back, a voluptuous warmth filled her that had nothing to do with the temperature of the air.

Without realizing how it happened, they were backed up against the car door giving each other kiss after earth-shattering kiss. She ran fingers through his vibrant black hair, reveling in the texture. Every part of him was perfect to her. He'd become her whole world. She welcomed him, obeying the needs driving her, never wanting this night to end.

Growing more uninhibited she kissed his cheeks, his throat, then returned to his mouth over and over again. As her euphoria deepened, a shudder shook his powerful body. The next thing she knew he'd buried his face in her silky gold mane, slowing down the sensual momentum.

"*Por Dios*, Jillian… This wasn't supposed to happen." His breathing had grown shallow. "I think we'd better get back to the casa."

"Not yet," she begged almost incoherently against those lips that had swept her away to a place she never wanted to leave. His Castilian face was so gorgeous she cupped it in her hands so she could kiss each masculine feature. He had no idea how being crushed against his body like this was thrilling her out of her mind.

"I don't want to go anywhere yet," she whispered, biting gently on his earlobe. "It's been such a long time," her voice shook. "Being out here with you like this has made me come alive. For a little while I want to make all the pain go away and just feel." She was bursting to tell him she loved him, but didn't dare yet.

His chest rose and fell noticeably, but she wasn't prepared for hands that had been caressing her hips to slide to her upper arms. His thumbs made circular motions against her skin, driving her wild with longing before he put her away from him none too gently. Those eyes, a dozen shades darker than the night sky, burned like black oil set ablaze.

"Maybe another time," he muttered. "Perhaps I didn't tell you the building contractor is going to be out first thing in the morning. He's meeting us at the mill house at eight."

She hadn't known what Remi was going to say, but that wasn't it. She'd hoped for some verbal indication that his feelings for her were growing, but apparently no matter how carried away she'd gotten, nothing was going to make him forget his pain.

Jillian had been the one to initiate what had happened out here. Just now he'd been the one to stop things from escalating out of control. For her to suggest they go on kissing each other had ended up being a major turnoff for him. With that mortifying conclusion sinking into her brain, she shook her head.

"I'm sorry. Now *I* feel the fool." She pasted a smile on her face and rubbed her palms against her jean-clad hips. "Kyle's death left me needier than I realized. As you said earlier, you've had a year longer than I to get a grip on your emotions. I promise this won't happen again."

Wheeling around she opened the passenger door and got in. Looking up at him she said, "Please say you'll put this little incident behind you. I don't want anything to interfere with our business relationship."

A pulse throbbed at his temple. "Nor do I."

Nothing could be plainer than that. The only way their arrangement was going to work was to keep everything on a professional basis. If she thought of him as Count Goyo and called him Senor, then it shouldn't be difficult.

Liar. Life was going to be another kind of hell for her now because the man who couldn't love her back was very much alive.

He shut the door and walked around to his side of the car. An uneasy quiet reigned inside until he'd turned on the headlights and they'd started back to the estate. "My intention in bringing you out here was to show you the windmills in case you wanted to include them on the tour bus itinerary."

How ironic. Here she'd hoped it was because he'd wanted to find them a secluded place to kiss her because he couldn't wait any longer to continue what had gotten started at the pool when he'd washed her hair.

You fool, Jillian.

The moment he'd brought his ex-wife into the conversation she should have figured out he was still in mourning for the stunning Letizia. The fact that he'd waited until his thirties to get married made her treachery all the more lethal and impossible to forget.

Three people had been out here tonight. Dave had warned Jillian, but her fearless nature had taken her where angels refused to go and she'd been forced to learn the devastating lesson for herself. The sooner she got it through her thick skull there could be no future with Remi, the better.

"It goes without saying a stop at Soleado Goyo will provide unexpected thrills for everyone. Thank you for letting me view them at such a bewitching hour. The light was perfect."

"I knew you'd appreciate their beauty."

She was about to say *who wouldn't*, then caught herself in time.

They drove the rest of the way in silence. As soon as he

parked the car in front of the main house, she alighted without his help. Always the gentleman, he saw her inside the foyer.

"Jillian?"

The blood pounded in her ears before she turned to him. "Yes?"

His eyes searched hers out of a face so shadowed it looked gaunt in the dim light. "I envy you your marriage."

But I'm not married anymore.

She'd thrown herself at Remi, yet tragically his scars ran so deep, he couldn't tell that she'd moved on. Was it because he was too scared to see it?

"Buenas noches, Senor."

Three weeks later the building contractor came to find Jillian in the newly remodeled olive press house. Early in the morning a delivery van had brought the first load of postcards and recipe booklets she'd had printed to sell along with the olive oil. The same label on the bottles appeared on the covers. The company she'd hired had done a wonderful job.

"Senora Gray?"

She paused in her work of putting the pamphlets on the shelf behind the counter and looked over at him. "Sí, Carlos?"

"Everything is finished. Do you want to inspect one more time?"

"I'd love to."

She left the olive press house and accompanied him to the other buildings. Between an efficient cleaning crew and a small army of construction workers, the entire complex had been transformed, surpassing her vision of how it would look when completed.

Though she had to function with an aching heart these days, she couldn't help but be thrilled to see that the plans she'd drawn up on paper for Remi had reached fruition. She'd only seen him coming and going while they did their respective work. There'd been no repeats of moments alone. Except for the times when they had to confer with Carlos about something, Remi had left her alone.

"You've restored the complex to a living museum the tourists will marvel over. *Muchas gracias*, Senor." The only thing lacking was the first busload of tourists destined to arrive on one of EuropaUltima's day excursions from Toledo. It would coincide with their grand opening scheduled in three days.

Carlos nodded in appreciation. "Don Remi told me to follow your ideas to the letter. Now I see why." He raised his index finger at her. "You are the one with the eye."

She smiled to herself. Since he didn't know about her bad eye, she had to take it as a compliment. "Between all of us, I think we've made a great team."

"Sí. Now if you will excuse me, I'm off to Madrid."

Madrid? "I thought you lived in Toledo."

"I do, but I'm driving there on business."

Her thoughts reeled. "Senor? If it wouldn't inconvenience you, could I possibly ride with you? I have an appointment there myself."

She knew she'd surprised him, but he hid it well. "Of course."

"Oh, thank you. I was going to ask one of the staff here on the estate, but if you're already going, I'll pay you for the gas."

"Why would you do that when I'm going there anyway? But I must leave soon."

"I'm ready to go now. Let me run back to the olive press house for my purse. I'll meet you at your car."

"Bueno."

This was a bit of luck she hadn't counted on. Knowing Remi's steel-trap mind, he was aware she needed to see Dr.

Filartigua again and would take the time off to drive her. With Carlos's help, she would be gone from the estate and thus avoid being alone with the Senor. That's what always got her into trouble.

Two minutes later she joined the other man and they drove out of the property through the other entry in the wall that had been reopened. It was perfect. No one saw them leave.

Most of the way to Toledo Carlos talked with various clients and family on his cell phone. That provided Jillian with the opportunity to call the doctor's office. The receptionist told her to come in at four that afternoon, their last appointment of the day. With that settled, Jillian rang the main house. Hoping she could be forgiven a little lie, she told Maria she'd gone on an errand with Carlos so Maria shouldn't expect her for lunch.

Maria always passed on any information to Remi. Hopefully he wouldn't think too much about it. Even if he did, which he probably would because that was his nature, it would be too late. She planned to stay at a hotel tonight, but not the Prado Inn. That was the first place Remi would call if he wanted to find her out of that misguided loyalty of his to Dave. Maybe she'd stay at one of the small hotels she'd seen near the pastry shop on the plaza.

If the doctor gave her permission to drive a car now, she could rent one tomorrow to drive back to the estate. She'd keep it for a week. It would give her back her independence while she shopped for a cheap second-hand car to buy. If she was going to be in Spain until December, she needed her own transportation for the hours she wasn't working. The key to surviving until then meant keeping as much distance from him as possible.

Remi and Juan were loading the truck with cartons of oil destined for the newly remodeled olive press house when he heard his cell go off. He checked the caller ID. When he saw Diego's name, he had to take it. The other man was making out the payroll. Once Remi cleared up his question, he got back to his task, but his ability to be civil to anyone was fading fast. Poor Juan hadn't said two words so far.

Lately Remi noticed everyone giving him his space, even Paco, who'd weathered the last two years with amazing understanding. Despite Remi's black moods that often lasted weeks at a time, Paco had managed to remain his friend. But in the last three weeks, Remi knew he'd hit a new low. Not even his foreman liked to be around him. Who could blame him?

His phone rang again. It was the janitorial service he'd hired from Arges. They called to say they were coming later in the day to give the new bathrooms from the converted storage shed a thorough cleaning. He gave them the go-ahead, but at this point he was ready to explode.

Every time his phone rang, he'd hoped it was Jillian needing him for anything at all, but since the night he'd come dangerously close to dragging her into the backseat of his car to make love to her, everything had been different.

Senora Gray had become the personification of the ideal business partner. No one worked longer hours than she did. Every night he found a detailed, precise summary of her daily activities in his e-mail. If she needed his input, she asked him to come to the olive press house at his convenience. She never complained. His house staff said they hardly knew she was around. The little girls adored her.

Remi couldn't handle the situation any longer.

He needed a knockdown, bare-bones talk with her until they both knew each other's truth! No holds barred.

Instead of sending Juan over in the truck with the cartons, Remi would go himself and surprise her on the job whether she liked it or not. In his gut he knew she wouldn't like it. That was too bad…

This morning he'd find out if she'd made her appointment with the doctor yet. If she could arrange for her checkup tomorrow, Remi would drive her to Madrid. They were both long past due a holiday from work. He'd take her out to dinner and they'd enjoy a night of flamenco, after which he'd get her into his arms and keep her there until she didn't long for Kyle anymore.

Until he applied the brakes that caused the truck to shimmy, he didn't realize how fast he'd driven to the olive press house. The force had probably knocked the cartons around. Muttering a curse, he jumped down from the cab and entered their new store expecting to find Jillian behind the counter with Soraya while they both got used to the new state-of-the-art register.

No one was here. The place was a tomb.

"Maldito!" he swore aloud before loading the hand truck to bring in the cartons. Once he'd finished, he strode swiftly to the mill house. Still no sign of her. She'd probably gone to the main house for lunch. He got back in the truck and started the motor. For the first time in a hellish twenty-one days he planned to join her for a meal.

A minute later he entered the kitchen through the back door. He thought he might find Jillian at the breakfast table. Once again he was disappointed. Maria nodded to him. She was on the phone.

Judging from the conversation, she was discussing the wine menu with the catering service from Toledo. Remi had hired them to prepare and serve the drinks and tapas to Maria's specifications.

While everything was still in the experimental stage, Maria

would run the minikitchen in the bar and Soraya would be the cashier. Jillian would be in charge of the store. Depending on how well things went after a few trial runs to work out the glitches, he'd hire and train permanent staff so his own house staff could get back to their normal lives.

He reached for a plum from the bowl. By the time she'd gotten off the phone he'd devoured it. "Is Senora Gray eating in her room or out in the patio room?"

"Neither. She went someplace with the contractor on an errand."

He frowned. "Carlos finished his work yesterday. I paid him last evening. What was he doing back here this morning?"

She shrugged. "Maybe to get a tool he left behind. They always do. What do you want for lunch?"

"Nothing right now, thanks. Do you remember when they left?"

"About two hours ago."

And they weren't back yet? He had a gut feeling something was wrong. He pulled out his cell phone. Before he spoke to Jillian he preferred to reach Carlos and find out what was going on.

While he waited for the contractor to answer, he walked outside so he could talk in private. Eventually the other man answered.

"Don Remi?"

"I understand you had to come back this morning," he began without preamble.

"Yes. The sign Senora Gray ordered for the wall behind the bar arrived. I put it up. Did you see it already?"

No, but then Remi's frame of mind had been so foul, he hadn't been looking for anything or anyone but her. "Not yet."

"She's a very clever woman."

Remi could tell the other man was just getting warmed up. She'd charmed every male on the property. After working with her three weeks, the contractor had a crush on her. What else was new?

"Where is she now, Carlos? Maria told me you two went on an errand."

"An errand?" He chuckled. "I suppose that's true. She asked for a ride to Madrid."

If Remi held the phone any tighter in his hand, he'd break it through brute strength. "Are you bringing her back?"

"Oh, no. She said she had business and would be returning to the estate tomorrow."

He should have anticipated something like this happening. "That was very nice of you to oblige her, Carlos," he said through gritted teeth.

"She's a very nice person. She explained she didn't want to put out anyone on the estate. Since I was going there, I was happy to take her. Would you believe she left a traveler's cheque on the seat for me? I'll mail it to you so you can return it to her."

"Keep it, Carlos. She's a woman who doesn't like to be indebted to anyone."

"Like I said, she's a very very nice woman. Very intelligent. Very beautiful. It's so sad about her husband. They were very much in love. Such a lucky man."

Stop talking, Carlos. Remi knew just how lucky Kyle Gray was. The pain of it had turned him inside out, the jealousy he felt burned deep. He bowed his head while he endeavored to get himself under control. "Did you drop her off at the Prado Inn?"

"No. She asked to be let out near the Plaza de Santa Ana."

"What time was that?"

"Twenty minutes ago. Is there a problem?"

A problem? *Sí, Senor*. It had to do with the whole rest of his life which wouldn't be worth a worthless *peseta* without her.

"No. It can wait until she returns." Except Remi wasn't going to wait. As soon as he showered and changed, he would go after her. "*Gracias* again, Carlos. You do great work."

"It's been a pleasure doing business with you, Don Remi. I plan to bring my wife to your grand opening on Saturday. *Hasta pronto*."

Three days away.

After Remi hung up, he phoned information for the Prado Inn and was connected, only to find out a Senora Gray hadn't checked in.

Not to be thwarted, Remi phoned Dr. Filartigua's office on the pretext that he would be meeting Senora Gray there, but he needed to be certain of the time so he wouldn't be late. The receptionist told him four o'clock.

Ten minutes later he got in his car and left the estate. En route he phoned Maria. "I'm on my way to Madrid. Phone me if there's an emergency. I'll be back later with Senora Gray."

CHAPTER NINE

ONCE JILLIAN had checked in to the Santa Ana hotel, she phoned the doctor's office to find out if they had a cancellation so she could get in sooner. After noticing that Remi had tried to reach her without leaving a message, she realized he'd already put two and two together. She couldn't handle seeing him right now. Tomorrow would be soon enough.

He deserved a medal for the way he'd stood in for Dave, but she didn't want that from him. She wanted his love, something he couldn't give.

The receptionist came back on the line and told her to come right over. The doctor would see her between patients. Jillian thanked her profusely and asked the front desk to ring for a taxi.

Within a half hour Dr. Filartigua had pronounced her fit to go back to her life and enjoy it. She gave him a hug before leaving the examining room. Though she doubted she'd ever get used to the dead spot in her eye, it was a small price to pay when she had her life.

"Senora Gray?" the receptionist called to her. "I forget to tell you that Don Remigio Goyo phoned earlier and I told him your appointment was at four o'clock."

So Jillian's instincts had been right. "That's no problem. Would you mind phoning him back and telling him not to bother to come in since I've already seen the doctor?"

"I'll do it right now."

"Do you have his number?"

"*Sí.*"

Her conscience was clear. Now there was no need to call Maria, either. "Thank you for fitting me in. You have no idea how much I appreciate it."

She left the office and walked across the street to the hospital, where there was a taxi stand. After she climbed in the back of the first car, she told the driver to take her to the Calle Serrano, where some of the best designer shops were located. Jillian hadn't bought a new outfit in months. With the grand opening on her mind, she wanted to wear something trendy, yet sophisticated. She'd buy a new pair of shoes, too.

By three o'clock she'd made her purchases, including a new frothy nightgown in peppermint pink with spaghetti straps that was sinfully expensive, but she felt like treating herself. Then she took a taxi back to her hotel.

After arranging for a rental car in the morning, she walked down the street to the pastry shop to celebrate the end of eyedrops and patches. One male customer seated at a table outside was eating something that looked mouthwatering. Jillian went inside to order the same dessert called *churros*, where sticks of fried dough were dipped into chocolate pudding. It was her second sinful purchase of the day, but she ate every bite and thoroughly enjoyed it.

Deciding she'd better burn off the calories, she took a long walk to the Royal Palace and spent time in the geometric Sabatini gardens to the north of it. Beautiful as they were, she would be content to feast her eyes on the Senor and his flower-filled courtyard for the rest of her life.

She ached for him. Somehow she'd thought that getting away from the estate for twenty-four hours would ease her longings. Instead the distance between them seemed to magnify her desire. Here she was in one of the great cities of Europe and all she wanted was to love him into oblivion.

Since those passion-filled moments out by the windmills, he'd left her alone. After the way she'd thrown herself at him, hadn't he thought about that night just a little bit? Most men wouldn't have been able to stay away from her, but then Remi wasn't like any other man.

She pounded her palm against her forehead. When was she going to realize those kisses he'd given her hadn't meant a declaration of love or anything close to it. Men were good at separating their emotions from physical needs. The women she knew had a harder time making the distinction, probably because they didn't want to.

Jillian was the kind of woman who couldn't give her all unless it meant forever. She'd given her all the other night. Remi was intelligent enough to know it, and brutally disciplined enough not to use her.

Despirited by the knowledge, she discovered she was tired and took a taxi back to the plaza. It was after 8:00 p.m. She bought two tapas and a drink from the Taberna to carry back to the hotel room.

For the first time in a month she was able to wash her hair herself. Though she would have loved to run all the hot water out of the shower, she was aware of the drought, so she made it quick. After she'd brushed her hair, she slipped into the nightgown and climbed on the bed to phone her brother.

He'd left his voice mail on. She called their land line. It

was on voice mail, too. She frowned. Maybe Angela was in the hospital having her baby! Her due date was next Monday, but that didn't mean it couldn't come early.

On a whim she got out the little notebook she kept in her purse and called Angela's sister, Pat. Her husband answered.

"Hi, Tom. It's Jillian."

"I guess you've heard," he said without bothering to engage her in conversation. She felt the first burst of alarm.

"What's wrong with Angela?"

"Dave didn't want you to know, but I guess you need to know now."

His remark triggered an old reaction. She started to shake. "Know what?"

"Angela's toxemia got so bad they had to do a cesarean section. Their baby boy is out of danger, but she's been in the recovery room all day while they closely monitor her for convulsions. It's touch-and-go right now. Pat's been there all day. All we can do is pray."

No…

This couldn't be happening again.

In the background she heard her hotel phone ring. "Just a minute, Tom. Maybe this is Dave calling now. I'll get back to you."

Frantic, she clicked off and picked up the receiver of the other phone. "Hello?" she cried anxiously.

"Jillian? What's wrong?"

"Remi—" She couldn't believe it. "H-how did you know I was here?"

"Never mind that now. Did the doctor find something else wrong with your eye? Is that why you sound so fragile?"

"No—" She hugged her free arm to her waist. "It's Angela. She had the baby, but I was just talking to her brother-in-law

Tom and he said she has toxemia. He said i-it's touch-and-go. If Dave and the children lost her…" Jillian was too upset to talk.

"I'm coming up."

Up? "W-where are you?"

"In the foyer. What's your room number?

"Twelve."

The line went dead.

Half a minute later she heard his rap on the door. She flew across the expanse to open it. Jillian didn't know how it had happened, but when she'd needed him most, there was Remi, holding out his arms. Again.

She ran into them, needing his solid warmth to cling to. He'd been her bulwark a month ago and was still here for her. One hand cradled the back of her head. The other roved over her back in a soothing motion while he whispered encouraging words. "She's going to make it, Jillian."

"She's *got* to. The children need her. My brother needs her. She's the sweetest wife and mom in the whole world. Oh, Remi, why do these things have to happen?" she sobbed the words. "I don't know how you found the strength to live through what you did."

He drew her tighter against him. "I found it the same way you did, the same way your brother will get through this."

"Deep down Dave's strong."

"Just like his sister."

"No, I'm not, but I've got to be strong for him now." She sniffed and finally pulled away from him. Her face still wet with tears, she said, "I'm sorry. I've ruined your shirt."

He was dressed in a black silk dress shirt and matching trousers. The man looked so incredibly handsome and substantial she had no words. Only then did she remember she'd answered the door in her nightgown. Though she was more than adequately covered, he'd caught her in a dark moment when she hadn't been aware of anything but her pain.

"Excuse me for a minute." She rushed into the bathroom and changed back into the skirt and blouse she'd put on that morning. When she returned to the other room Remi was on her cell phone to someone. His shuttered black eyes followed her progress as she walked over to him.

"Your brother's on the line."

Those were the exact words Pia had said before Jillian had said hello and learned the ghastly news that Kyle had been killed. She didn't think she could live through another tragedy this soon.

Her ears started to ring as she took the receiver from him. Through wooden lips she whispered, "Dave?"

"Angela's out of the woods!" he cried happily. "I know what Tom told you, but the worst is over. She's going to be fine and we have our Matt. Seven pounds fifteen ounces, twenty-one inches long."

"It's a miracle. Thank heaven," she murmured, but so much joy after so much fear caused her to weave.

By now Remi was holding her up. He took the phone from her lifeless fingers.

"Jillian will call you right back. Congratulations again to you and your wife, David." He rang off, then picked her up and carried her over to the chair, where he sat down and cuddled her against him like he would a child.

She'd gone limp as a noodle, yet slowly but surely his warmth permeated her limbs. In a few minutes strength returned to her body. He always knew what to do to make her feel better. Her thoughts started to string together again. All of a sudden a light went on and she became cognizant of the fact that she was sitting on his lap as if she had every right.

Disturbed by this recurring weakness to cling to him, she raised her head and started to get off his lap, but he held her in place with those strong hands. "Don't move yet. Give yourself a chance to get over the shock."

Jillian was already over the first shock of the evening. Angela and the baby were going to be fine. That was all she needed to know. It was the shock of finding herself in this position with Remi that was making her unsteady now. She'd promised to maintain a professional demeanor with him, but as usual she'd slipped under her own radar.

It felt too good to rest against his chest and feel the pounding of his heart beneath her hand. She found every inch of him so appealing, she was in danger of making a fool of herself again. With the slightest provocation she would cover his mouth with her own and never let him go. But she couldn't do that.

Summoning every ounce of moral fiber she possessed, Jillian slid off his thighs and stood up. The room had grown dark. She turned on a lamp and looked for her sandals. Once she'd put them on she felt less vulnerable.

While he lounged in the chair with his long powerful legs extended, he looked relaxed yet she knew his body was always on the alert for the slightest irregularity where she was concerned.

His fiery black gaze swept over her. As she felt him take in every detail, she quickly subsided into the other chair, which was propped next to the table where she'd put her food and soda. She wanted answers to certain questions but didn't know where to start.

"How long have you known about Angela's toxemia?"

"Since I phoned your brother while you were being operated on."

She nodded. "Now it makes sense why he didn't come."

Remi leaned forward. "The man was torn up. Both women in his life needed him."

"If Angela hadn't needed him more, I know he'd have been at my side in a flash, but when you get married, you vow to forsake all others. That's the way it should be, the way it *has* to be to make it work."

"Agreed."

No man had more proof of that than Remi, but she couldn't let his pain sway her from what had to be said.

"I need to talk to you about something important."

He cocked his head. "In what regard?"

She took a struggling breath. "I'm angry with you, Remi."

"I'm already aware of that," came the level response.

"I mean it!" she cried. "You lied in order to protect me from worrying about Angela. Worse, to keep your promise to Dave that you'd watch over me, you purposely let me believe you wanted to use my idea to give you another source of income. To top it off, you've let me use your casa as my own personal hotel under the guise of helping Carlos catch my vision."

She jumped to her feet, unable to sit still. "Don't you know what you've done?" Her question reverberated against the walls. "How am I supposed to handle the fact that a stranger I almost killed has sacrificed *everything* for me? I can't bear it that you've spent your hard-earned money on a project that would never have been your idea in a million years and might not work."

A stillness infused with tension surrounded them before he said, "Are you through?"

Jillian wanted to shake him. "No!"

She reached for her purse and opened it to get out her checkbook. "I saw the final bill when Carlos wasn't looking. After adding up all the services you'll have to pay for to get my idea off the ground, the total sum is *not* as negligible as you would have me believe.

"Therefore," she said as she sat down again and wrote him out a check, "this is my contribution to our business arrangement. Kyle left me with enough insurance that I can afford this. If you don't deposit it in the morning, then I'm walking out on you before the grand opening without any compunction whatsoever." She got up and dropped it in his lap.

He eyed her narrowly. "I'll do better than that. Forget renting a car and come home with me tonight. I'll deposit your check at the bank on our way out of the city. If it hasn't closed, I'll give you the receipt as proof. Perhaps you've forgotten we have an early morning appointment with the fire chief, who's going to inspect the premises and make certain we're up to fire code."

As a matter of fact she *had* forgotten. Her hands shook as she closed her purse. "In another life you'd have made a top secret agent, Senor."

Remi laughed without mirth. "None of us escape our fate." On that cryptic note he got up from the chair. "Since you left without luggage, I trust you don't have a great deal to carry out to the car."

His gaze took in the packages on the bed before settling on the sack. He looked inside. "Aren't you going to eat these?"

She shook her head. "I had a huge dessert a few hours ago and I'm still digesting."

"*Churros*, I believe."

Jillian let out a self-derisive laugh. "I thought I was being so clever."

One black brow quirked. "Carlos used that very adjective to describe you. Knowing how much you enjoyed the tapas and marzipan the last time we were in Madrid, I made inquiries and was able to track you down."

"You're too cagey by far!"

He chuckled before eating both tapas. "The doctor's office called to let me know you'd gone in early for your appointment. Then when you didn't check in to the Prado Inn or the Zalacain, where your tour buses stop, I figured you must have returned to the scene of the crime. The rest was simple logic." He popped the lid on the can and drank all of it without taking a breath.

She started to gather up her things.

"Don't forget that nightgown you were wearing. I realize it wasn't meant for my eyes, but for what it's worth, I'm still reeling."

Maybe he was, but he'd get over it. Men did…

Five minutes later Jillian had canceled the rental car and settled her bill. They drove away from the hotel. True to Remi's word he headed straight for the bank he patronized.

She watched him put her check in the night deposit. Just knowing she'd taken the first step to pay him back for his goodness to her, helped her to relax. If she were honest with herself, she had to admit she much preferred being with him than having to drive the rental car alone tomorrow. But at the same time it defeated her plan to be totally independent of him.

"Now that you're able to drive again, I'll give you one of the estate cars from the plant. That way you can come and go when you want."

Sometimes he was so in tune with her thoughts it was scary. "Thank you. That's very generous."

"It's a necessity."

He was probably relieved he wouldn't have to chauffeur her around anymore.

She felt him dart her a glance. "After our grand opening, feel free to take some time off to fly home to your family. I trust it's a reunion you all need."

The thought of leaving him for any reason made her heart lurch. "Luckily Angela's parents and siblings are there to help out. I'll wait and see when Dave wants me to come." Pathetic creature that she was, Jillian was still holding out the hope Remi might go with her.

The car ate up the kilometers. "Are you getting hungry?" They'd reached the outskirts of Toledo.

"No, but I bet you are. Those two tapas were hardly a drop in the bucket for you."

"I can wait 'til we get back home."

He loved his home. So did she. "Remi?" she whispered.
"Sí?"

"I realize you take all your responsibilities seriously, especially me. I—I didn't mean to upset you today by leaving the estate with Carlos. It's just that I hated the idea of you having to take me to the doctor again. You've already done so much."

She heard him breathe in deeply. "Did it ever occur to you I like a break now and then?"

"Well, of course, but it must be getting tedious ferrying me back and forth to Madrid."

"Madrid has the best nightlife in Spain. I'd hoped to take you to one of my favorite haunts, but plans have a way of changing."

Jillian gave him a covert glance. "You were there when I needed you tonight. I'm beginning to think you really are my guardian angel." Except that would mean he wasn't mortal. She couldn't stand the thought of Remi not being flesh and blood.

A few months ago she'd read a paranormal novel about a man who'd been sent from heaven to save lives. She hadn't been able to get all the way through it because she kept thinking about Kyle, wishing there'd been some supernatural power to save him.

"Even though you're angry with me?" he challenged.

She exhaled the breath she'd been holding. "Even though."

They were getting closer to the estate. Jillian didn't want this time to end. "Remi, do you mind if I ask you something personal? Of course you don't have to answer if you don't want to."

"I thought you would have done so long before now. Your forbearance is another exceptional trait I find refreshing. What is it you want to know and I'll do my best to satisfy your curiosity."

After another nervous wiggle she said, "Were there other women before Litizia?"

"Dozens."

Jillian couldn't tell if he was teasing or not, but he probably wasn't. "How is it you didn't marry until your thirties?"

"With dozens, why bother?"

Beneath his glib response she sensed he wasn't lying. So far Jillian was the last one in a very long line.

"Will you be serious for a minute?"

"So you want the whole truth and nothing but."

"Do you think I can handle it?" she quipped.

"Then here it is. I never found a woman I loved more than myself."

Jillian burst into laughter. "Your honesty is refreshing, Senor." But deep down his answer killed her. After waiting for the right woman all that time, and then to realize he hadn't really known her…

"Letizia dazzled me, tricking me into believing the world started and ended with her. Once the honeymoon was over I discovered what selfishness can do to a marriage. Once my feelings for her began to die, I couldn't resurrect them. We didn't have relations for the last four months of our marriage. It was no way for either of us to live. The divorce came as a relief."

Before the night was over she needed to ask one more

question. In this rare, confiding mood, he might give her the answer. "Did you catch her and Javier together?"

"No," he said without hesitation. "I came back to our bedroom from a day's work and saw a note propped on the dresser. She said she'd gone away with Javier, who gave her the love I couldn't."

A woman spurned? Was that the way Letizia had turned things around when she discovered she couldn't dangle Remi on the end of her finger any longer?

What the Senor had just told her couldn't possibly be all of it. Jillian knew there was more to the story than maybe even he knew about, but she'd pried enough for one night. While she was looking blindly out the passenger window she saw a flash. It came from her right eye.

There it went again.

She tried to contain her panic, but she couldn't hide anything from Remi who put his hand on her arm. "What's wrong?"

"I'm seeing flashes out of my bad eye."

A low chuckle came from his throat. "That's because we're experiencing dry lightning tonight."

Dry lightning?

"You're kidding! I've heard of it before, but I've never seen it. Thank heaven. I thought my eye was having problems." Relief washed over her in waves. "But Remi— there's no storm."

"It's up there, but the clouds are so high the water evaporates before it ever reaches the ground."

He slowed the car so they could watch. Several cars had done the same thing.

A series of lightning bolts over the olive groves illuminated the sky. The wait between bolts didn't take long.

"If this keeps up those trees are going to catch on fire."

"One already has," he muttered. "I've got to get back." He

floored the accelerator and they flew the last few kilometers to the estate.

Adrenalin surged through her. "How do you put them out?"

"We don't, but the roads between the groves act as a natural fire break if the wind isn't too strong. Mostly we watch in case the fires start to get too close to human habitation."

She shuddered to think of La Rosaleda being destroyed.

When they turned in at the gate, several of the workers were already gathered in their cars ready to ride out. Remi drove her to the front of the main house. He jumped out of the car and hurried around to help her. Paco was beckoning him over to the truck.

"You go on, Remi. Be careful," she cried.

For one brief moment his eyes blazed into hers before he climbed in the cab with his foreman and they took off. If she'd had the temerity, she would have asked to go with him, but she couldn't put him in that position in front of the people who worked for him. Instead she had to wait here and worry until he came back.

After she'd put her things away in the bedroom, she walked through the casa to the kitchen. She found Maria at the table having a cup of tea. The other woman smiled at her.

"On nights like this, no one sleeps. Come and join me."

Jillian took a banana from the bowl and sat down to peel it. "You seem so calm."

"This happens every summer. Fortunately there's not a lot of wind tonight. They'll be back soon."

"Remi will be hungry and exhausted."

"I made food earlier. All you have to do is warm it up."

After a month of working together, Jillian had grown close to Maria and liked feeling a part of things. "I should have told you where I was going with Carlos today. I just didn't want o be a burden to Remi again, but as it turned out, he drove to Madrid to find me when he should have been here with a storm brewing." She got up to put the banana peel in the wastebasket.

"You should have seen his face when he couldn't find you."

Jillian eyed Maria frankly. "That's because he made a promise to my brother to take care of me. Today I didn't make t easy for him."

Maria took her empty cup to the sink and washed it out. "Perhaps not. The difference is, when his wife left him, he didn't go after *her*."

"She didn't go alone, Maria."

"Remi loved the estate. Javier loved the city. The only reason he stayed as long as he did was because he didn't want to let his brother down, but there comes a point when a man has to follow his destiny."

"If he wants to be happy," Jillian murmured. He'd said the same thing to her during the drive home tonight, but he'd been talking about himself.

"Remi's been in a dark place for a long time. So dark, he couldn't see that Javier was never interested in Letizia. That one was born to cause trouble."

Jillian was thunderstruck. "Are you saying she lied about her involvement with Javier?"

"I've worked for the Goyo family for twenty-two years. I know what I know."

"But the note she left Remi… He thinks they were lovers!" she cried out aghast.

"Both brothers have too much pride. The Goyo men are known for it. But just remember, they have their sweet mother in them, too. *Buenas noches*, Jillian."

"*Buenas noches*, Maria."

After she left, Jillian stood at the counter remembering the look of pain on Javier's face. She believed Maria.

Now to get Remi to believe it. There was work to be done.

She went to the fridge and rummaged inside for different items of food she knew he liked. After putting it all together on a large plate, she covered it with foil. When he came back, he'd be ravenous.

Once everything was done, she went to the bedroom to freshen up and brush her hair. A little floral spray, a fresh coat of pink lipstick and she was ready. Knowing Angela and the baby were all right had put a spring in her step. Though she knew Remi would crave sleep when he returned, she'd never felt more alive. It was her turn to wait on him and let him know what it was like to be cherished.

Another hour passed before she heard the front door open and close. She hurried to the foyer to greet Remi only to find that Paco had come in alone. It was difficult if not impossible to hide her disappointment.

"Was it bad out there, Paco?"

"Not so much." He drew a can of beer from the fridge. Before she knew it, he'd swallowed all of it. "We only lost ten trees tonight."

Ten—that sounded bad to Jillian.

"Where's Remi?"

The other man threw the empty can in the wastebasket. "He went home."

She bit her lip. "I have his dinner ready."

He gave her a quick smile. "I'm sure he wouldn't mind if you took it to him."

Jillian had never been to his house. He'd never asked her.

In the next breath Paco grabbed an apple from the bowl and bit into it. "*Duermes bien*, Senora."

CHAPTER TEN

REMI HAD BARELY walked in his house when he heard knocking on the front door.

It was after 2:00 a.m. He heaved a weary sigh. Since the storm had long since passed over, there was no more threat of fire tonight. It had to be Paco with some minor emergency.

He retraced his steps to the foyer and turned on the light. When he opened the door, the shock of seeing Jillian robbed him of words. She might have been an apparition standing there with her golden hair brushing against her shoulders. Those iridescent eyes gleamed.

More times than he could count he'd wished she would have sought him out here, but it would have to be of her own volition and he'd given up that hope.

"I realize you must be dead on your feet, but you need to eat first. I brought you dinner." For once she'd caught him completely off guard.

"I need a shower before that."

"You do." Her full-bodied smile beguiled him. "You smell of smoke. If you'll let me come in, I'll wash the ash out of your hair."

Maybe he'd gotten too close to the fires and was hallucinating. It made him so slow on the uptake she moved past him and shut the door. "I'll give you two minutes to change into your swim trunks and get in the tub before I invade your bathroom. Afterwards I'll serve you dinner in bed. I'm starting to count now." Remi had never moved so fast in his life. By the time she called out, "Ready or not," he'd managed to wedge himself in the tub he rarely used because he preferred showers. But not tonight, *madre de Dios*, not tonight!

While the water was filling the tub, she entered his bathroom as if she'd done it every day of her life. Somewhere along the way Maria's shopping bag had been left behind. She plucked his shampoo from the stall, then looked down at him as if he were a puzzle.

"You're going to have to lie down. Those big feet will have to rest up against the tiles."

He stared into her eyes. "Better watch out or you'll get wet."

"I expect to."

"Don't say you weren't warned."

Having more fun than he'd had in the whole of his life, he went under and felt half the water spill over the sides. When he came up for air she was kneeling next to him. Her fragrance took him back to the moment at the crash site when he'd lifted her body from the driver's seat. In the last thirty days there'd been such a drastic change in his world, Remi didn't know himself anymore.

He watched in fascination as she poured the gel in her feminine hands, but the second he felt her fingers plunge into his wet hair, he couldn't keep his eyes open. The sensation was divine beyond description.

"Never stop," he begged. She was working his hair into a lather while massaging his temples and behind his ears.

"Enjoying it, are you?"

His lips curved. "What is it you want? Name it and it's yours."

"You should never make promises like that, Senor. One day I may ask you to deliver."

"Why not right now?"

"You've given me a lot to think about. I need time to decide what I want most."

"Give me a time frame."

"After the grand opening?"

"I've already told you I want you to visit your family, so it has to be something else."

"It will be. Now I think it's time for your rinse. I'll start your shower."

He grasped her left hand. "Don't leave me yet."

"If I don't, you're going to become solidified in suds."

Remi sat up. "How about a neck rub. I swear I won't ask for anything else." At least not in here.

"I'll be happy to oblige, but I need both my hands first."

Remi kissed the end of each dainty finger before letting her go. He peeked at her through his lashes. Their faces were on eye level. Hers was flushed like the wild red roses overhanging the portico.

As she kneaded his nape and shoulders, his heart virtually clapped against his ribs. She finished by giving him a brief kiss at the top of his spine. It arced to every atom in his body. Much sooner than he liked he heard water running.

"Don't take too long or your food will get cold."

Needing her like he needed life, he showered quickly and pulled on his toweling robe. After using a hand towel to absorb the runoff from his hair, he tossed it aside and walked into his bedroom.

She'd turned down the bed covers. With a pat to the mattress she said, "Come and get in."

He moved to the bed and sat back against the headboard.

She covered his legs with the sheet. "Can I expect this service every night from now on?"

Jillian refused to look at him. "Only when there's a special need."

"As in?"

"Fighting fires." She drew out a foil-covered plate from the bag.

"I watched it with the men. There's a big difference."

"Not to me." She set it on his legs and pulled off the foil. Next came his utensils wrapped in a napkin. "Firefighters get killed on fire watches."

His heart started going crazy. "You thought I wasn't going to come back?"

"Sometimes people don't.' She shot him a look that melted his insides. If she was saying what he thought she was saying…

"I don't plan to go anywhere until I'm an old man. It's too good right here." He started eating.

She rubbed her arms as if she didn't know what to do with them. He knew what he wanted her to do with them.

"Maria was so calm about it."

"She comes from a farming family near Cáceres. It's nothing new to her."

Jillian reached in the bag once more. "I didn't know what you wanted to drink so I brought two different kinds." She put both cans on the bedside table.

"Both will do nicely." He reached for the beer. "You drink the grape juice and we'll toast our new venture."

Remi raised his can. As she lifted hers to clink his, he shook his head. "In order to do this right, we have to wrap arms and drink from each other's cans."

A smile lit up her face. She leaned closer and entwined her arm with his.

Together they drank a little. Above the rim of her can he saw the outline of her pear-shaped pupil. The sight was precious to him.

When she lowered her arm, he couldn't resist kissing the mouth that had given him ecstasy three weeks ago. For the first time in a month he didn't feel that anyone was here but the two of them. If he was wrong, he didn't want to wake up from this enchantment.

She moved away and stood up to drink her juice. "It's your bedtime, Senor. We have to be up early, remember?"

He was one step ahead of her. "The fire chief joined us tonight. He said to expect him tomorrow afternoon. That means we can all sleep in. Stay with me tonight," he whispered.

She averted her eyes. "That's a very tempting offer, but after the grueling day you've had, you need sleep and nothing else. I happen to know you worry too much about everything and everyone. Tonight I give the *Conde* permission to take a vacation from himself."

Just now she'd turned *him* down, verifying his deep-seated fear that though her attraction for him was strong, she still couldn't let go of the past. Maybe she'd never be able to. A grunt came out of him to cover his pain. "Am I really that bad?"

Her gaze finally met his. "Worse," she declared with that innate honesty of hers. "So I'm going to say good-night. *No dejes que la cama errores mordida.*"

Don't let the bedbugs bite? "Who taught you that?"

"Marcia."

Remi laughed until long after he'd closed and locked the front door after her.

Jillian checked her watch. It was 3:30 p.m. At four o'clock the bus would be arriving. She needed to be out in front of the barn to greet everyone and introduce them to Paco. He would give the tourists a tour of the olive groves before they returned to the mill house for tapas and drinks. This trial run had to go better than well, not only for EuropaUltimate Tours, but for Remi.

She hadn't seen much of him since the other night when she'd daringly washed his hair in the bathroom of his own gorgeous casa. The way she'd behaved, she might as well have worn a sign that read Take Me. I'm Yours. To her chagrin the Senor was a superb poker player because he hadn't treated her any differently than usual.

After leaving his elegant house, a smaller version of La Rosaleda, life had gone on as normal. If he'd wanted a repeat performance, there'd been no indication.

However, she couldn't think about that right now. All her efforts needed to be focused on tonight's big event.

Jillian had bought the perfect outfit for the evening. The black, knee-length trapeze dress was pin-tucked with a buttoned high collar and full sleeves caught at the elbow. The sheerest hose and strappy black sling-back heels completed the picture.

She'd used the dryer on her hair so it curved slightly at the shoulders from a side part. For the first time since coming to the *casa* she made up her eyes and wore a deeper rose lipstick that went well with her skin tone.

In truth Jillian had dressed fit to kill for her host tonight. She'd even bought a new rose-scented perfume for the occasion. A dab or two was enough.

One more item to go. Before leaving the room she pinned the EuropaUltimate Tours identification tag to her right shoulder. She hadn't worn it in five weeks. For six years her work as a guide had consumed her, but since she'd had this time off, it felt strange to be official again. Remi's world had changed her.

He's become my life. The realization shook her to the core. If she hadn't had the accident, they would never have met.

Her injured eye no longer represented loss and pain. It represented a rebirth. If this business venture turned out to be as successful as she hoped, maybe Remi would be able to see enough daylight to rid himself of his demons and really look at what was standing before his eyes.

She dashed through the house and out the front door to the car where Remi was lounging against the fender with a small box in his hand. He'd dressed in a formal midnight blue suit. His monogrammed tie with the Goyo coat of arms flapped against his dazzling white shirt. He was so handsome it literally hurt her heart. She thought he looked more royal than Juan Carlos.

In the process of devouring him with her eyes, she didn't realize he was taking all of her in with equal intensity. Neither of them spoke. It was as if a spell had been cast over them. She watched him swallow before he opened the box and lifted out a corsage of deep pink roses.

How did he know what color to pick? He never failed to astound her with his thoughtfulness. The two of them seemed to be in some incredible dream. He gravitated to her and pinned it on her left shoulder.

"*Jillian…*" His voice shook. She could tell something profound was going on inside him. He grasped her upper arms almost as if he needed support. "The day of the accident Diego said it best. Senora Gray has the kind of beauty to strike a man dumb."

Nice as that was to hear, she didn't want to strike him dumb. She wanted to hear what was inside his heart!

"That's because you're all dark-haired around here, but I appreciate the compliment. Thank you." Trying to tamp down the pain she said, "I think—I hope we have an audience waiting."

As his jaw tautened, his gaze dropped to her high heels. "I'll drive us over."

"I can walk there."

"Not this evening," came his gravelly voice.

A strange tension encompassed them as he helped her into the car. Before he started the motor he turned to her with a sober expression. "I once accused you of having a deceptive shell."

Why bring that up now? "Did you? I'd forgotten."

"I said it at the height of your pain. It was cruel," he muttered in self-abnegation.

"Your wife gave you reason to be cynical." She heaved a sigh. "Remi? Do you know what I wish?"

His eyes grew tense and watchful.

"Forgive yourself for being human so you can be happy again." *So you can love again. I want you to love* me.

As her plea resonated in the car's interior, the seconds ticked away. He gave her thigh a squeeze before turning on the motor. While electricity raced through her body he drove them around the main house to the complex. The caterers had arrived.

Everyone else on the staff had assembled. Soraya's little girls were dressed in new outfits. They looked darling. Jillian flashed Remi a glance. She was so nervous for everything to go right, she was feverish. Now that the tour bus had come, no telling how many people would show up for the grand opening scheduled for an hour from now.

"Remi?" His head jerked around, meeting her gaze head-on. "You won't mind if I introduce you this one time? This is our maiden voyage. The impression we make tonight will be the most important one. Every person on that bus including the tour bus personnel will tell everyone they know how fantastic Soleado Goyo is. Word will spread like wildfire. Before you know it, you'll be able to buy back the rest of the olive groves."

"Jillian—" Again he started to say something to her, but Paco had opened the door on Remi's side.

"The bus is coming through the gate."

Her eyes met Remi's. "This is it. *Vamanos*!"

Paco chuckled at her funny Spanish accent, but not her brooding host. After she jumped out of the car, Remi cupped her elbow and walked her over to the barn. Soon they saw the bus coming down the track beneath the trees. It pulled to a stop in front.

Jillian waved to Otto, one of the drivers she knew well. Soon Francine and Telly, longtime guides, stepped off the bus.

"Jilly—Wow! Don't you look terrific! I'm green with jealousy."

"Don't be silly."

While they hugged, Telly walked right up and kissed Jillian on the lips. "Hey, babe. I think somebody made it up about you being in a car accident. You're looking hot," he whispered.

Out of the corner of her eye she saw Remi grimace. He had no idea all her coworkers goofed around like this. Her poor Senor was so proper and she loved him so much!

"Why don't you guys tell your group to get off the bus and I'll introduce you to everyone."

Francine nodded. "Got it."

Watching twenty-four tourists—thin, big, short and tall, old and young—pour out of the bus brought back hundreds of memories. Yet again Jillian had the feeling that being a tour guide like Francine was all behind her.

Jillian stepped forward. "Welcome to Soleado Goyo, ladies and gentlemen. Their extra virgin olive oil carries that brand name that literally means 'sunny,' because the sun is captured in every delicious bottle.

"You're in for an experience of a lifetime. My name's Jillian, and as you can see by my name tag, I'm an employee of EuropaUltimate Tours.

"Before we do anything else, I'd like to introduce you to Count Remigio Alfonso de Vargas y Goyo, a descendent of the Duke of Toledo and the present day owner of this fabulous estate. If it weren't for him opening up his doors to this part of his ancestral home, this tour wouldn't be possible."

As cameras clicked and flashbulbs went off, the oohs and aahs coming from the awed group assembled was a very satisfying sound. She didn't dare look at Remi right now. He didn't like to use his title, but this was one time when it was going to pay dividends in spades!

"And now I'd like you to meet Paco Avilar, who knows more about the olive tree and the making of virgin olive oil better than any man alive except Count Goyo. He'll accompany you on the bus around the property and take you through the olive oil-making process. Ask him anything. This will take approximately an hour.

"If you need to use a restroom before you go, do so now. They're behind the mill house to my right. Any of you who need a soda or bottled water are welcome to buy one inside the olive press house to my left. Paco's daughter, Soraya, and his son-in-law, Miguel Gutierrez, and their two daughters, Marica and Nina, will be there to assist you.

"Your tour will leave in ten minutes. When you return, you'll be able to enjoy dinner in our tapas bar inside the mill house run by Paco's wife Maria before your return to Toledo."

Some of the group dispersed, but most had gravitated to Remi as Jillian knew they would. He was so gorgeous no one could look anywhere else. The women acted starstruck and the men were scratching their heads trying to figure out how such a man existed. She knew exactly what was going through everyone's minds. Remi was better-looking than any movie star. Besides being Castilian, he was a real count.

Francine took her aside. "Good grief, Jilly. How in the hell—pardon the French—did you find him?" She'd locked her jaws so her voice wouldn't carry. "He's drop dead superfabulous. I've been coming to Spain for ten years and I never in my life saw anyone like him."

"It's a long story."

She eyed Jillian with speculation. "Something's going on between you two. The vibes are practically tangible. He hasn't taken his flashing black eyes off you once!"

"Oh, Francine." She laughed quietly. "It's good to see you." She hugged her again. "Thanks so much for the flowers."

"I'm glad you liked them. Everyone's been wondering how long it would take for you to start living again. I can tell from the light in your eyes you're happy. That's the best news of all. By the way, how's your eye?"

"It's fine."

"Which one got injured?"

"Can't you tell?" Jilly opened them wide.

"Well I'll be darned if your right pupil doesn't look like a comma."

Jillian started to laugh. At the sound, Remi strolled to her side. "What's so funny?" he asked in his deep voice near her ear.

"Francine says my pupil looks like a comma, and I think it looks like a green pepper. What do you think? Come on." She smiled up at him. "You can tell me. I've been dying to know anyway."

Remi's lips twitched. "A pear."

Francine nodded. "I can see that. Let's get Telly's opinion."

He came out of the olive press house with a bottle of water. When Francine explained what they were doing, he walked over to Jilly and stared into her eyes. "Felix the Cat without ears."

"That's stretching it, Telly."

The other man hugged her extra hard, letting her know without words he was pulling for her. After he let her go, he said, "We need you back. How soon are you coming to work again? I've got plans for us."

Don't say any more, Telly. Remi doesn't know you're just having some fun with me.

"December first." It killed her to say it, but it was time to face the truth.

He frowned. "Why so long? Doctor's orders?"

This time Remi's jaw had an unmistakably aggressive thrust.

"N-no," she stammered. "I'm staying on here until then in order to make certain all the quirks are worked out. I wouldn't want Don Remigio to regret opening up his estate for EuropaUltimate Tours."

Francine must have sensed certain undercurrents and turned to Remi as if realizing he needed to be appeased. "The company is terribly excited about this addition to the Spanish itinerary, Count Goyo. Trust Jilly to have been the one to make it happen. With her in charge, you have nothing to worry about."

"I second that," Telly interjected. "Every year we get more business because of her."

Remi gave an imperceptible nod before staring into her eyes with an enigmatic gaze. "I can believe it."

Jillian would have given anything to know what he was really thinking, but the tourists had returned to the bus talking animatedly. A very good sign already. Some of them asked her questions, drawing her attention away from Remi before they climbed on board.

Paco filed on after the tour guides, giving Jillian and Remi a rueful grin as the door shut. She watched the bus leave for the olive groves, all the time aware of negative tension emanating from Remi.

There was a yawning silence that filled her with anxiety. "Have you forgiven me for putting you in the limelight?" she teased in the hope of breaking through his forbidding facade.

Ever since Telly had kissed her, she'd felt a change in Remi. He couldn't be jealous. That would imply his emotions were involved, that he was in love. If that were the case he would have asked her to stay on the estate forever, as his *wife*! He'd had plenty of chances. In fact he could have told her that the other night, but no such words had passed his lips.

"There's nothing to forgive," came his wooden response. "I'll be back after the tour bus has left the estate to see if the bar is doing any business." He headed for the car.

"Where are you going?"

"Does it matter?" he called over his broad shoulder.

"You *are* angry." Without thinking, she chased after him and got in the front seat at the same time he did. "Tell me what's wrong."

"Get out of the car, Senora Gray."

Once she might have been intimidated by his treatment of her, but no longer. Something earthshaking was going on inside of him and she intended to get to the bottom of it. "If you want to get rid of me, you'll have to unstrap me and lift me out bodily, but I'm warning you now I'll go kicking and screaming."

In a jerky motion he started the engine and drove along the road leading to the gate where the bus had passed through. Within seconds they were out on the highway leading south.

For the next five miles Jillian pored over the list of reasons for the drastic change in him on the most important night of their lives.

"Remi…" Her mouth had gone so dry she could hardly talk. "I—I really didn't think you'd mind my introducing you by your title."

"The title be damned," he bit out. "There's something much more important at stake here." That remote, unreachable look had broken out on his dark face.

Heartsick she cried, "Was it too much of an invasion? Do you wish we hadn't done this?"

The faint white ring around his lips frightened her because she didn't know what emotions were causing it.

"What is it?"

When there was no answering response, she realized the problem went much deeper than anything that had happened tonight, yet something about her conversation with Telly had triggered it.

Her thoughts darted back to a certain conversation with Maria. *You should have seen the look on Remi's face when he couldn't find you. When Letizia left him, he didn't go after her!*

Jillian was convinced Maria had been trying to tell her something vital that night.

Was Remi upset because she'd told Telly she would be leaving in December? Had he been hoping she would never leave, but needed her to go after him now?

In the distance she saw the turnoff for the village of Arges. Taking the biggest risk of her life she said, "Remi? I'm afraid all the excitement has given me a headache and I don't have any painkillers with me. Would you mind stopping long enough to get me some?"

Drawn out of that dark place by her unexpected request,

he darted her an anxious glance before slowing to negotiate the curve. In a matter of minutes he'd found a *farmacia* on a quiet street and had come back to the car with pills and some bottled water. They were virtually alone.

"Thank you." She shook out two and swallowed them, glad for the water to take away the dryness of her mouth.

"Is the pain coming from your eye?" The deep concern in his voice gave her all the impetus she needed to follow through with her plan.

She screwed the lid on the half-drained bottle and put it in her lap before looking at him. "I'm in pain, but it isn't coming from my eye." Continuing to stare at him she said, "The other night after I washed your hair, you told me you would grant me anything I wanted. If you recall, I said I would let you know what I desired most once the grand opening was over."

His answer to that was to breathe more heavily. At least she had his attention now. Summoning up every ounce of courage she continued.

"But I've decided it can't wait that long because I'm so in love with you I can hardly breathe and, when you can't breathe, it's painful! The truth is, what I want most is to be your wife and love you forever."

"Jillian—"

The emotion that came out with the sound of her name gave her the answer she'd been waiting for.

"It's true, darling. When Telly put me on the spot tonight, I hoped you would intervene and tell him you would never let me go away. I can't stand any distance that separates us."

So saying she leaned across the gearshift to reach him. He moved faster and drew her all the way into his arms, crushing her against his hard, trembling body. With his face buried in her hair, he whispered the endearments she'd longed to hear.

"I planned to ask you to marry me tonight, *amorada*, but after you told your colleagues you were leaving in December, I was terrified you meant it and I needed to be alone to come up with a new strategy to keep you here."

"Don't you know I love you, Remi?" she cried. "This hopeless, one-eyed American who almost killed you and roped you into a business arrangement wants all of your body, mind and soul," she whispered against his lips before kissing him with a ferocity of passion already spiraling out of control.

"I'm a very greedy, possessive woman who can't wait to be Senora Goyo and bear your children. Our time has come if you have the courage to take me on."

He kissed her with a savagery she couldn't get enough of. "Your bravery and beauty enslaved me the moment I lifted you from the car and laid you on the ground. By the time the helicopter arrived, I was determined to make you mine no matter how long it took."

She covered his face with kisses. "I've been in love with you since the hospital." She held his face between her hands and drew it down to her. "I'll be the first one to admit I never thought I could love again, but when I woke up from the operation, there you were at my side. I knew I was going to be happy again. I don't know how I knew it. I just did.

"Kyle will always be in my heart and you'll always have those first memories of falling in love with Letizia, but they belonged to another world. You and I collided in this one. I have a bad eye to prove it."

She stared into his eyes. "You're the most wonderful man I've ever known. I love you so much, Remi. Maybe one day you'll realize I'm never, ever going to go away."

"*Mi corazon.*" He crushed her against him, burying his face in her neck. "Ever since you came to my house the other night, I've been out of my mind wanting you, loving you. I have to marry you as soon as possible. I don't want to live through any more nights without you in my bed."

"Will you use your title to arrange for a special license so we can be married right away?"

"I'm way ahead of you. We'll get married on the estate tomorrow and honeymoon in New York. I want to meet your family."

Joy swept through her.

"We'll phone them with the news after we close up shop tonight." He rocked her in his arms. "Would you think I was terrible if I told you I'm thankful for that bull?"

"So am I, darling. I fear we might never have met otherwise. You would have turned me down on the phone."

"I don't know. There's something about you that drew me from the very beginning. All I know is, I couldn't live without you now. I swear when I found out you'd gone to Madrid with Carlos, my world caved in until I found you."

"I was hoping you'd come after me," she confessed. "When you told me you were in the hotel lobby I began to think maybe I was going to get my heart's desire after all."

There was only one shadow marring their future now.

"What about your brother, Remi? I had a talk with Maria the night of the fire and—"

"I know," he whispered against her lips, stifling the rest of her words. "She told me about it the next day. He's been trying to talk to me for a long time. I'm finally ready to listen. I invited him to come and have a drink with me at the Holy Toledo tonight."

"You did?" she cried for happiness.

"It's all because of you, darling. I'm ready to let the world know how I feel about you. I want you to meet him. I love my brother, Jillian."

"Of course you do. He loves you, too. I could see it in his eyes the day we bumped into him in Madrid."

Remi nodded. "For two years I've loathed myself for jumping into marriage with a woman I hardly knew. She was capable of anything, especially the lie she wrote to me in that note. Unfortunately I took everything out on Javier. He never did like the olive oil business, yet I refused to accept it."

"You've accepted it now. You're over the worst part. The best is yet to come."

The desire in his black eyes was eating her alive. "You're the best thing that ever happened to me. I'll never let you go," he vowed.

Jillian couldn't take in all her joy at once. She held him tighter as their mouths fused in ecstasy. Right now she was unable to find the words to express the depth of her love. For the moment it was enough to be held in the arms of her very own man of La Mancha.

* * * * *

Turn the page for a sneak preview of
AFTERSHOCK, *a new anthology*
featuring New York Times *bestselling author*
Sharon Sala.

Available October 2008.

n o c t u r n e ™

Dramatic and sensual tales of paranormal romance.

Chapter 1

October
New York City

Nicole Masters was sitting cross-legged on her sofa while a cold autumn rain peppered the windows of her fourth-floor apartment. She was poking at the ice cream in her bowl and trying not to be in a mood.

Six weeks ago, a simple trip to her neighborhood pharmacy had turned into a nightmare. She'd walked into the middle of a robbery. She never even saw the man who shot her in the head and left her for dead. She'd survived, but some of her senses had not. She was dealing with short-term memory loss and a tendency to stagger. Even though she'd been told the problems were most likely temporary, she waged a daily battle with depression.

Her parents had been killed in a car wreck when she was twenty-one. And except for a few friends—and most recently her boyfriend, Dominic Tucci, who lived in the apartment right above hers, she was alone. Her doctor kept reminding her that she should be grateful to be alive, and on one level she knew he was right. But he wasn't living in her shoes.

If she'd been anywhere else but at that pharmacy when the

robbery happened, she wouldn't have died twice on the way to the hospital. Instead of being grateful that she'd survived, she couldn't stop thinking of what she'd lost.

But that wasn't the end of her troubles. On top of everything else, something strange was happening inside her head. She'd begun to hear odd things: sounds, not voices—at least, she didn't think it was voices. It was more like the distant noise of rapids—a rush of wind and water inside her head that, when it came, blocked out everything around her. It didn't happen often, but when it did, it was frightening, and it was driving her crazy.

The blank moments, which is what she called them, even had a rhythm. First there came that sound, then a cold sweat, then panic with no reason. Part of her feared it was the beginning of an emotional breakdown. And part of her feared it wasn't—that it was going to turn out to be a permanent souvenir of her resurrection.

Frustrated with herself and the situation as it stood, she upped the sound on the TV remote. But instead of *Wheel of Fortune,* an announcer broke in with a special bulletin.

"This just in. Police are on the scene of a kidnapping that occurred only hours ago at The Dakota. Molly Dane, the six-year-old daughter of one of Hollywood's block-buster stars, Lyla Dane, was taken by force from the family apartment. At this time they have yet to receive a ransom demand. The housekeeper was seriously injured during the abduction, and is, at the present time, in surgery. Police are hoping to be able to talk to her once she regains consciousness. In the meantime, we are going now to a press conference with Lyla Dane."

Horrified, Nicole stilled as the cameras went live to where the actress was speaking before a bank of microphones. The shock and terror in Lyla Dane's voice were physically painful to watch. But even though Nicole kept upping the volume, the sound continued to fade.

Just when she was beginning to think something was wrong with her set, the broadcast suddenly switched from the Dane press conference to what appeared to be footage of the kidnapping, beginning with footage from inside the apartment.

When the front door suddenly flew back against the wall and four men rushed in, Nicole gasped. Horrified, she quickly realized that this must have been caught on a security camera inside the Dane apartment.

As Nicole continued to watch, a small Asian woman, who she guessed was the maid, rushed forward in an effort to keep them out. When one of the men hit her in the face with his gun, Nicole moaned. The violence was too reminiscent of what she'd lived through. Sick to her stomach, she fisted her hands against her belly, wishing it was over, but unable to tear her gaze away.

When the maid dropped to the carpet, the same man followed with a vicious kick to the little woman's midsection that lifted her off the floor.

"Oh, my God," Nicole said. When blood began to pool beneath the maid's head, she started to cry.

As the tape played on, the four men split up in different directions. The camera caught one running down a long marble hallway, then disappearing into a room. Moments later he reappeared, carrying a little girl, who Nicole assumed was Molly Dane. The child was wearing a pair of red pants and a white turtleneck sweater, and her hair was partially blocking her abductor's face as he carried her down the hall. She was kicking and screaming in his arms, and when he slapped her, it elicited an agonized scream that brought the other three running. Nicole watched in horror as one of them ran up and put his hand over Molly's face. Seconds later, she went limp.

One moment they were in the foyer, then they were gone.

Nicole jumped to her feet, then staggered drunkenly. The bowl of ice cream she'd absentmindedly placed in her lap shattered at her feet, splattering glass and melting ice cream everywhere.

The picture on the screen abruptly switched from the kidnapping to what Nicole assumed was a rerun of Lyla Dane's plea for her daughter's safe return, but she was numb.

Before she could think what to do next, the doorbell rang. Startled by the unexpected sound, she shakily swiped at the tears and took a step forward. She didn't feel the glass shards piercing her feet until she took the second step. At that point, sharp pains shot through her foot. She gasped, then looked down in confusion. Her legs looked as if she'd been running through mud, and she was standing in broken glass and ice cream, while a thin ribbon of blood seeped out from beneath her toes.

"Oh, no," Nicole mumbled, then stifled a second moan of pain.

The doorbell rang again. She shivered, then clutched her head in confusion.

"Just a minute!" she yelled, then tried to sidestep the rest of the debris as she hobbled to the door.

When she looked through the peephole in the door, she didn't know whether to be relieved or regretful.

It was Dominic, and as usual, she was a mess.

Nicole smiled a little self-consciously as she opened the door to let him in. "I just don't know what's happening to me. I think I'm losing my mind."

"Hey, don't talk about my woman like that."

Nicole rode the surge of delight his words brought. "So I'm still your woman?"

Dominic lowered his head.
Their lips met.
The kiss proceeded.
Slowly.
Thoroughly.

* * * * *

Be sure to look for the AFTERSHOCK anthology
next month, as well as other exciting paranormal stories
from Silhouette Nocturne.
Available in October wherever books are sold.

nocturne™

NEW YORK TIMES BESTSELLING AUTHOR

SHARON SALA

JANIS REAMES HUDSON
DEBRA COWAN

AFTERSHOCK

Three women are brought to the brink of death...
only to discover the aftershock of their trauma has
left them with unexpected and unwelcome gifts of
paranormal powers. Now each woman must learn to
accept her newfound abilities while fighting for life,
love and second chances....

Available October wherever books are sold.

www.eHarlequin.com
www.paranormalromanceblog.wordpress.com

SN61796

SPECIAL EDITION™

BRAVO FAMILY TIES

Tanner Bravo and Crystal Cerise had it bad
for each other, though they couldn't be more
different. Tanner was the type to settle down;
free-spirited Crystal wouldn't hear of it.
Now that Crystal was pregnant, would
Tanner have his way after all?

Look for

HAVING
TANNER BRAVO'S
BABY

by *USA TODAY* bestselling author
CHRISTINE RIMMER

Available in October wherever books are sold.

REQUEST YOUR FREE BOOKS!

2 FREE NOVELS PLUS 2
FREE GIFTS!

HARLEQUIN ROMANCE®

From the Heart, For the Heart

YES! Please send me 2 FREE Harlequin Romance® novels and my 2 FREE gifts (gifts are worth about $10). After receiving them, if I don't wish to receive any more books, I can return the shipping statement marked "cancel". If I don't cancel, I will receive 4 brand-new novels every month and be billed just $3.32 per book in the U.S. or $3.80 per book in Canada, plus 25¢ shipping and handling per book and applicable taxes, if any*. That's a savings of over 15% off the cover price! I understand that accepting the 2 free books and gifts places me under no obligation to buy anything. I can always return a shipment and cancel at any time. Even if I never buy another book, the two free books and gifts are mine to keep forever.

114 HDN ERQW   314 HDN ERQ9

Name	(PLEASE PRINT)	
Address		Apt. #
City	State/Prov.	Zip/Postal Code

Signature (if under 18, a parent or guardian must sign)

Mail to the **Harlequin Reader Service:**
IN U.S.A.: P.O. Box 1867, Buffalo, NY 14240-1867
IN CANADA: P.O. Box 609, Fort Erie, Ontario L2A 5X3

Not valid to current subscribers of Harlequin Romance books.

Want to try two free books from another line?
Call 1-800-873-8635 or visit www.morefreebooks.com.

* Terms and prices subject to change without notice. N.Y. residents add applicable sales tax. Canadian residents will be charged applicable provincial taxes and GST. Offer not valid in Quebec. This offer is limited to one order per household. All orders subject to approval. Credit or debit balances in a customer's account(s) may be offset by any other outstanding balance owed by or to the customer. Please allow 4 to 6 weeks for delivery. Offer available while quantities last.

Your Privacy: Harlequin Books is committed to protecting your privacy. Our Privacy Policy is available online at www.eHarlequin.com or upon request from the Reader Service. From time to time we make our lists of customers available to reputable third parties who may have a product or service of interest to you. If you would prefer we not share your name and address, please check here. ☐

HR08R

Harlequin® Historical
Historical Romantic Adventure!

HALLOWE'EN HUSBANDS

With three fantastic stories by

Lisa Plumley
Denise Lynn
Christine Merrill

Don't miss these unforgettable
stories about three women who
experience the mysterious
happenings of Allhallows Eve
and come to discover that finding
true love on this eerie day is not
so scary after all.

Look for
HALLOWE'EN HUSBANDS

Available October
wherever books are sold.

HARLEQUIN Romance.

Coming Next Month

**Handsome sheep barons, maverick tycoons and dashing princes—
you can find them all in Harlequin Romance®!**

#4051 BRIDE AT BRIAR'S RIDGE Margaret Way
In the second of the *Barons of the Outback* duet, Daniela Adami comes to Wangaree Valley to escape her life in London. Her heart is guarded, but when handsome sheep baron Linc Mastermann strides into her world, he turns it upside down....

#4052 FOUND: HIS ROYAL BABY Raye Morgan
Crown Prince Dane—the third of the *Royals of Montenevada*—has heard rumors of a secret royal baby. With the kingdom in uproar, his only choice is to confront Alexandra Acredonna—the woman who still haunts his dreams....

#4053 THE MILLIONAIRE'S NANNY ARRANGEMENT Linda Goodnight
Baby on Board
The only thing businessman Ryan Storm can't give his six-year-old daughter is a mom—but he can hire the next best thing.... Pregnant and widowed, Kelsey Mason isn't Ryan's idea of the perfect nanny—but little Mariah bonds with her straight away, and soon he starts to fall under her spell....

#4054 LAST-MINUTE PROPOSAL Jessica Hart
Cake-baker Tilly is taking part in a charity job-swap, but when she's paired with ex-military chief executive Campbell Sanderson, Campbell is all hard angles to Tilly's cozy curves. But something about her always makes him smile. And then they share a showstopping kiss....

#4055 HIRED: THE BOSS'S BRIDE Ally Blake
9 to 5
Mitch Hanover needed a miracle—someone to bring life to his business—and when Veronica Bing roared up in her pink Corvette and told him she was the girl for the job, he couldn't help but agree! But even though attraction zinged between them, Mitch had sworn never to love again....

#4056 THE SINGLE MOM AND THE TYCOON Caroline Anderson
Handsome millionaire David Cauldwell is blown away by sexy single mom Molly Blythe. He can see she and her young son need his love as much as he yearns for theirs—but falling in love means taking risks: David must face the secret that changed his life....

HRCNM0908